GHOST AT THE PROM

GHOST ORACLE BOOK 4

BY ROGER HYTTINEN

RAMBLING WORDSMITH PRESS

By Roger Hyttinen

ISBN: 978-1-943005-38-3
(Paperback edition)

Roger wishes to thank you for reading his work. Please consider leaving a review wherever you purchased this book. Also consider telling your friends about it to help me spread the word about my book.

Webpage:
https://rogerhyttinen.com

LICENSE NOTES

CHAPTER ONE

"SOMETHING WEIRD IS GOING ON," Nick said, taking a swig of his warm Coke. The fizzy bubbles caused him to crinkle his nose. "There are a lot more ghosts around than usual."

He, Gabe, and many of their classmates were sitting outside during lunch to take advantage of the warm sunny day. It had been a long, chilly winter in Gallowspine Mountains, so even the slightest hint of spring was enough to send everyone running outside during lunch—especially with the school year nearly over.

"Oh, yeah?" said Nick's boyfriend, Gabe. "Like how many ghosts are we talking about here? A hundred? Two hundred? Five hundred? A thousand? Twenty thousand?"

Nick punched Gabe in the arm. "Stop sassing me, boy."

Gabe flashed Nick his infamous half-grin. "Some days, I just can't help myself. But seriously, how many more of them are you seeing? You used to notice them only now and then, right?

"Yeah. At most, one or two a day. But now they seem to be everywhere, and it's becoming more and more difficult to ignore them, especially since so many of them seem so lost and confused. There's definitely something strange going on with the Other Side."

Some egg salad dribbled out of Gabe's sandwich. He scooped it up with this index finger and licked it off. "Do you think it has anything to do with that 'ol shadow demon that your psychic friend's been talking about?"

Gabe was referring to Nate, an acquaintance of Nick's deceased uncle. According to Nate, there is an unknown entity who's blamed for the recent deaths of several psychic mediums in Europe. Nate advised that all mediums should neither acknowledge nor assist any spirits that they come across. Nick was finding it increasingly difficult to ignore the ghosts, especially when many of them seemed so desperate. It tugged at his heart to do nothing when he could be helping...should be helping.

Nick creased his brow. "Could be. Last I heard from Nate, a group of psychics from all over Europe were meeting in France at a conclave to try and figure out a solution. I wish I could go."

"How cool would that be?" Gabe said. "Imagine going to France and hanging out with a bunch of European psychics. What do you say? Perhaps we can save up enough money to go."

Nick chuckled. "Yeah, keep dreaming, buddy. That is so not gonna happen. Do you have any idea how expensive it is to fly to Europe? Even if my job would let me put in some overtime—which they wouldn't — we'd never come up with enough funds by the time of the meeting."

"When is it?"

"Only a few weeks away, I do believe. I sure hope they can figure this thing out. I know that I'm supposed to try and stay under the radar of this shadow thing, but it's not easy ignoring the ghosts. It doesn't help that it's getting more and more difficult for me to tell them apart from the living. I recall my uncle saying that the longer they stay earthbound, the more they begin looking like normal people."

"So, you haven't talked to any ghosts since that incident with the Burtons?"

Nick shook his head. "Not a one. I promised Katrina that I wouldn't until the psychics can figure out exactly what or who it is that's killing mediums."

"Good answer," said Gabe. He locked eyes with Nick. "Especially since you promised me as well."

Nick felt himself melting into Gabe's gaze, but then snapped his head away. Ever since they'd confessed how they felt about each other, Nick had found it almost impossible to keep his hands off of his boyfriend. He didn't want his feelings for Gabe to appear too obvious at school. Keeping his feelings for Gabe a secret was almost as difficult as hiding the fact that he could see ghosts. But the one thing that he didn't need was for his and Gabe's secret getting out around school. He'd seen firsthand how mean some of his fellow students can be.

Nick nodded and slurped the last of his Coke through the straw. "No worries. A promise is a promise."

"And if by some chance you did somehow manage to get involved with a ghost, you'd make sure that I was involved too, right? No secrets between us?"

"No secrets." Nick discretely rubbed his hand down Gabe's back. "We're a team, now."

Gabe smiled. "By the way, when are you gonna teach me those Tarot cards of yours? You've been promising me for a while now, but I've yet to see a single card come my way."

"I didn't think you were actually serious about that."

His eyes gleamed. "Hell yeah, I'm serious. Who knows? Maybe I'll be a natural and give you a run for your money."

Nick rubbed his chin. "How about tomorrow after school?"

"Why not today?"

Nick shook his head. "I gotta work today. I've missed so much work because of the last ghost case that I'm afraid I'd get into trouble if I miss any more. I'm scheduled off tomorrow, though."

Gabe held up his cup in a mock toast. "Tomorrow it is then."

Nick smiled and looked away. He turned his gaze to the back door of the school and noticed a girl standing there, staring intently at him and Gabe. He looked away.

"What's up?"

"It appears as though I might have inadvertently caught the attention of a ghost."

"Oh, shit. Where is it?"

Nick gestured with his head. "Standing by the door of the school."

Gabe looked to where Nick gestured. "You mean that girl in the short black jacket?"

"You can see her?"

"Of course I can see her. That's Ericka Spooner."

"Ah. So she's not a ghost." Nick breathed a sigh of relief. He should have known that the girl wasn't a ghost as he didn't get the usual physical reactions that gripped him whenever a spirit was nearby.

"Not as far as I know. She was in my Biology class."

"Have any idea why she's staring at us?"

Gabe shook his head. "Not really. I've only talked to her a couple of times. You know, I believe she was at Eterna last weekend when we were there. I kinda remember her staring at us then, too."

"Maybe she's crushing on you."

"Or on you."

Gabe glanced over at her again. "Uh-oh. It looks like she's headed this way."

"You're Gabriel, right?" She stood at the far end of the picnic table, shrugging off her jacket and draping it casually over one arm. Her light blond hair was neatly combed back and tied with a dark red ribbon that stood out like a streak of paint. Her eyes—an intense forest green—held just a flicker of orange near the pupil. A thin gold bracelet dangled from her left wrist, its delicate charms catching the light with every movement. She wore a fitted white top and dark jeans so deep in color they could have passed for black. Nick thought that she might be one of the prettiest girls in the school.

"Yeah, but most people call me Gabe."

"Gabe it is, then. I'm Ericka." She turned her gaze to Nick. "I think I've seen you around."

Nick nodded. "Me too," he said, even though he had no recollection of seeing her before today. "I'm Nick."

"Mind if I join you?"

Gabe shot Nick a quick glance and then shrugged. "Sure."

She wobbled a bit as she swung her leg over the bench, and Nick noticed that she was wearing bright blue heels that were about three inches high. She was fashionable as well as beautiful. She clasped her hands in front of her on the table and seemed to study Nick and Gabe, giving them a long, slow once-over.

"So how long you guys been boyfriends?" A half-smile played on the edge of her lips.

Nick felt the red creep up his face. "You mean how long we've been friends?" He looked at Gabe, who stared at him wide-eyed. "I dunno, about four years."

"Shortly after I moved here from Kentucky," Gabe added. "That's almost five years ago."

"Nice try fellas, but I can tell that you're more than friends. You're dating, aren't you?" Her eyes narrowed as she met Nick's stare. This was not good. She was the kind of girl that would get all up in your business and then tell the entire school. How could she have known about him and Gabe? Were they being too obvious at school? Shit, shit, shit.

Before he could object again, Gabe butted in. "How d'you know?" His voice was a little above a whisper. "Are we that blatant?"

She laughed. "Nah, I wouldn't have figured it out. But I saw you guys at the coffee shop last weekend. The way you were talking to and looking at each other, it was obvious that something was going on between you. Dudes don't look at each other like that unless they're hooking up."

Nick saw the panic in Gabe's eyes. He took a deep breath. "We're not....you won't tell anyone, will you?" Nick said.

She rolled her eyes. "Of course I'm not going to tell anyone. But I want you to do me a favor?"

"Sure," said Gabe. "Anything."

Oh crap, Nick thought. She's going to friggin blackmail us. He leaned forward, stiff and tense.

She had a devilish look in her eyes. "Oh, relax. I'm not going to shake you guys down or anything like that. All I want is for you to take me to the prom."

Gabe stared at her, all aghast-like. "Who, me?"

"Both of you," she said and laughed. "Or do you already have dates?"

Nick eased back, surprised, then coughed to suppress an inappropriate laugh. "No, we weren't planning on going. But how are both of us suppose to go with you? And more importantly, why? I'm sure any guy in the school would be more than happy to take you to the prom."

"And herein lies the problem," she said. "I want to go to the prom with my girlfriend, but she won't go as my date. She's not ready to come out yet, and frankly, neither am I. But she agreed to go if I can find us dates who won't spend the entire evening groping us, and you are the perfect guys to play that part."

"You're gay?" asked Nick. "But you're gorgeous!"

Gabe gave him the stink eye, and Ericka chuckled. "Thanks....I guess. Yeah, I'm a lesbian." She held out her hand, palms up in a 'voila' gesture. "And yes, even the hot ones can be gay."

Gabe laughed. He leaned in closer to Ericka. "So tell us, who's your girlfriend?"

"She doesn't go to this school. She goes to the public school."

Nick wasn't quite on board yet with the idea of going to the prom, especially with Gabe. Not that he wouldn't love to go to the prom with Gabe. He would. But like Ericka said, he's not ready to come out at school, and kids might talk if they showed up together, even if they had girls as their dates. Sounds too risky.

"So how 'bout it?" she asked. She put a hand on Nick's arm. "Will you do it?"

Gabe gave Nick a 'so-what-do-you-think' look, and Nick shrugged. "I dunno. I'm not much of a prom guy, and to be truthful, I'm not sure I want to risk it. People aren't stupid. They might easily put two and two together."

"Look," she said, with a crestfallen look on her face. "You guys have nothing to lose. You won't know anybody there, so who cares if anyone figures it out? And it's not like we'll be making out or anything. None of us wants our secret to get out, so it goes without saying that we'll be as convincing as possible as two hetero couples." She gave Nick a tight-lipped smile. "We'll even chip in for your tux rentals."

"Wait...so you're not talking about the prom at our school?" Gabe asked.

Ericka shook her head. "Oh, hell no. Tana has this thing about going to the prom at her school. It's super important to her for some reason. If it weren't for her, I wouldn't even go. But she's pretty insistent. She said that if I can't find us a date, then she'll go with one of the boys from her school." She narrowed her eyes and almost glared at Nick. "Now we can't be having that, can we?"

Nick reared back. "I suppose not."

Her eyes brightened. "So, you'll do it then?"

Gabe looked at Nick and shrugged. "I'm okay with it if you are," Gabe said.

That'd at least get him off the hook in case anyone at his school should ask him, as unlikely of a scenario as that would be. Nobody would be expected to pay for and attend two proms. The only downside was his parents. He'd planned on coming out to them eventually, and he feared that going to the prom with a girl would only give them the wrong impression. He'd have to deal with that later.

"Sure, I guess I'm game," Nick said.

She clapped her hands with delight and then raised

both hands in victory. "Fantastic! I'll tell Tana to sign us up."

"Your girlfriend's name is Tana?" asked Nick.

Ericka nodded. "Tana Stadden."

"Are we going to have to like...get you corsages or something?" asked Gabe. "Isn't it a tradition, right? We'd have no problem with that, mind you. I just don't know how this all works, given that I've never been to a prom before."

"I'll make you a deal. How about if you both get each other flowers or beer or whatever gay boys like to give each other, and Tana and I will exchange our own. Less stress that way."

"Works for me," Gabe said.

"Never figured that I'd be going to the prom," said Nick. "Am I going to have to dance?"

Gabe raised his eyebrows. "I don't think I even know how."

Ericka shook her head. "Not if you don't want to. Tana's not much of a dancer either."

"When is the prom?" asked Gabe.

"Two weeks."

"Two weeks! That doesn't leave us much time," said Nick. "What all do we have to do?"

"I'll take care of enrolling us," said Ericka. "You'll need to rent a limo, make dinner reservations, and rent tuxes."

"Yikes!" said Gabe. "Sounds expensive."

"Not to worry," said Nick. "I have some cash tucked away. But there goes our France money."

"You two are going to France?" she asked.

Gabe laughed. "Not really. We were only pretending. Let me get your cell number so we can keep in contact if need be."

They exchanged phones and typed in each other's numbers. "So, who's going with whom?" asked Nick.

Ericka winked at him. "You're a cutie. I'll be your date. I'm a sucker for curly hair."

"Hey!" said Gabe. "He's mine."

She chuckled. "For show only." She nodded to Gabe. "I think you'll like Tana. She's Southern too."

Gabe perked up. "Oh yeah? Where's she from?"

"Florida."

"We don't really consider Florida the South. I mean it is, but it isn't. Just like Atlanta isn't really Georgia."

"Whatever," said Ericka. She checked her phone. "I have to get to next hour's class. Text me if you have any questions about the prom." She gave them both a warm smile. "I appreciate you guys doing this for us and don't worry—we'll have a blast. Plus, I hear that the after-prom parties are big fun."

"There are after-prom parties?" asked Nick.

"Don't you know anything?" said Gabe. "The post-prom parties are legendary. They're the main event of the evening. That's when everyone gets lucky, you know." He winked at Nick and then wiggled his eyebrows for emphasis.

"Really?" asked Nick.

"So I've heard," said Gabe.

"Huh," said Nick. "I guess I'm a bit out of the prom loop." He smiled. "Though truth be told, it's never been much of a priority of mine. Until now, that is."

"Atta boy," Ericka said. She waved. "And Nick, how about getting a teensy-weensy haircut before prom?"

"What's wrong with my hair?"

"Nothing, babe," said Gabe. "I love it just the way it is—bushy and all. But a little trim never hurts anyone."

NICK HEADED to the janitor's closet right after class, ready to get to work. As soon as Nick opened the door, the foul stink of cigarette smoke attacked his nostrils, indicating that his boss Frank had recently burned one in the room, despite the school's No Tolerance policy and the supposed Tobacco-Free Campus initiative. Nick was surprised to see Frank standing there waiting for him. Usually, Nick was lucky if he ran into the guy once a week. The man had a large orange stain on his coveralls as though he had dropped a plate of saucy spaghetti on his chest.

"Hey Frank," Nick said.

Frank nodded and furrowed his brow. "Nick. Glad I was able to catch you. I need to talk with you."

Alarm slipped up Nick's spine. He tried to think back as to whether he'd screwed up at work, but nothing came to mind. His job was reasonably straightforward—clean all of the bathrooms on each floor and sweep the hallways. Which he always did. Well, except for that one time—but that wasn't his fault given that a creepy ghost with half his face missing scared the bejesus out of him. Not that he could tell that to Frank.

"You remember that you were hired for this job through the Community Action Agency, right?" asked Frank.

"Yeah. It's funny. I'd almost forgotten that I'd signed up with them when they called. I was lucky to get this job. I remember them saying that they had a huge waiting list of kids looking for jobs, and it could be quite a while be I'd hear back from them. It did take several months before they contacted me with an offer."

Frank ran his fingers through his hair. "You see, Nick, here's the thing. Because it's a community-funded organization, I have to make a monthly report for all the employees hired through them." He took a deep breath. "Were you aware of their attendance policy?"

Uh-Oh. Nick had a pretty good idea where this was heading. "I don't recall hearing anything about it."

"It was supposedly in the packet of info that they sent to you. In summary, you are allowed to miss no more than four shifts during a month—at least that's what the lady who called told me. Said it's stated in the contract that you signed with the agency." He paused. "Um...so...last month, you missed eleven shifts, Nick."

Nick had been so caught up in the last ghost case he'd been working on that he didn't even think about the possibility of getting into hot water at work. When he was first hired, Frank had told him that as long as he found a replacement or called in, he wouldn't get into trouble. He didn't recall anything about an attendance policy.

Frank closed his eyes for a moment and then reopened them. "So I figure you know what this means."

"You're firing me?" Nick felt a flush of embarrassment run up his face. Nobody had ever fired him before. He felt a mixture of outrage and humiliation. What was he going to tell his parents? They were gonna be so pissed.

"Someone from the agency called me this morning and told me that I was to relieve you of your duties effective today. Someone else will be taking your place immediately."

Nick nodded but said nothing. The anger drained from his body, and a sadness crept in. A heavy lump rose in his throat. His attention focused on the steady drip, drip, drip of the sink behind him. He'd been meaning to tell Frank about the leaky faucet.

"Gosh darn it, Nick, I hate to do this. You know that, right? You're a good kid, and you do good work. But dammit, my hands are tied on this one. The job is through the agency, not through the school, so there's not a whole lot I can say about it one way or another." His right foot repeatedly bounced on the floor. "I suppose you could try and appeal to the agency, maybe talk to someone there. I know you've had a couple of deaths in the family recently. They might take that into consideration."

"So today's my last day?"

Frank shook his head, giving Nick a sad look. "Sorry, Nick, but yeah. I can't let you work today. It's really shitty this is, but there's not a damned thing I can do about it." He broke his gaze from Nick. "If you have any personal items here, make sure to take them with you."

Frank rose and rubbed his neck. "Do you have any questions or anything about what I told you?" His voice was unusually soft when he spoke. "I'm supposed to ask you that."

"I don't think so," Nick stammered. "So that's it then? I'm done?"

"Afraid so." He reached out his hand, and Nick shook it. "It's been great working with you, kid. Sorry it had to end this way."

"You too," said Nick. He rose and left the room, finding himself in the middle of the long, empty school hallway. He leaned against the row of orange lockers and sat down on the cold cement floor. He lightly banged his head against a locker, surprised at how much noise it made. Getting himself fired from his job was not good news, given that he'd just committed himself to going to the prom. He had a little bit of money stuck away but had still counted on his paycheck continuing for the next couple of weeks. He doubted that his parents would front him any cash, especially given that he had gotten fired from his job.

He then thought about his friend and mentor Katrina, who owned a New Age shop downtown, where she also provided private psychic readings to customers. Maybe she could use some extra help at the shop after school or might know someone who had a job. He glanced at his phone. She didn't close for another hour and a half, so he'd have plenty of time to get there. He crossed his fingers, hoping that if she didn't have a job for him, she might at least know someone who did.

Once outside, he unlocked his scooter and fifteen minutes later, arrived at Katrina's shop. The parking lot next to the building was nearly empty. He parked his scooter next to a blue Jeep.

He jerked open the door, his entrance announced by the gentle tinkling of the bell above the doorway. Katrina was leaning on the counter, reading a thick hardcover book when he entered the store.

"Nicholas! What a surprise." She creased her brow. "Is everything okay? Shouldn't you be in school?"

He nodded and brought out his best smile. "I'm fine."

"No ghost encounters?"

Nick shook his head. "There're plenty of ghosts around, more than I've ever seen. But I've been taking your advice and have avoided all contact. It's been weeks since I've talked to any of them."

"Good. Have you heard from your French friend? Is there any news about what or who this shadow demon might be?"

"The last I heard was that there was a huge meeting planned with all of the European psychics about how to get rid of it." He smiled. "Hey, maybe you should go!"

Katrina chuckled. "As much as I would adore a visit to the City of Lights, traveling to France is far beyond my budget at the moment. We'll see what they determine at the meeting and then take it from there." She snapped the book shut and shoved it beneath the counter before Nick had a chance to see what it was. "So, what brings you here?"

Nick sighed. "I lost my job today."

She straightened, and her green eyes bore into him. "Oh Nicholas, I'm so sorry. What happened?"

"I got fired for missing too much work."

She nodded. "Not surprising. I was wondering if you were going to get into trouble for that. You do have to admit that you were calling in fairly often for a while there."

"I know. But I didn't call in once this month, now that I'm avoiding ghosts. You'd think they'd have taken that into consideration."

"Have you told your parents yet?"

Nick shook his head. "I just found out a few minutes ago." He paused. "Plus, I wanted to talk to you first."

"Me? About what?"

"I was wondering if you needed any help here at the store."

She studied his face for a couple of moments. "I wish I could hire you. I can barely support myself with the money that this store brings in. It seems like everyone's buying their supplies and books online these days. If it weren't for readings, I'd starve to death."

"Do you know anyone else who might be willing to hire a high school kid who can see ghosts?"

Her brows slid together as if in deep thought, and then she gaped at him. Her face brightened, and a spark of interest lit her eyes. "Of course!" She clapped her hands excitedly. "I have an absolutely marvelous idea, Nicholas." Her lips tightened into a mischievous smirk.

"I'm all ears."

"You could do readings here at the shop."

Nick swallowed, not liking at all the way the conversation was going. "I don't think I could do that. No way."

"Why not? You're a natural."

"I could never read for strangers. First off, I'm no expert. I mean, what if the reading is wrong? I could misinterpret the cards. I have in the past."

She chuckled. "Nobody is ever one hundred percent right. But from what I know of you, you're right much more often than you're wrong."

"That's because I get it directly from the mouths of ghosts. I don't know anything about reading for strangers."

She reached over and touched his arm. "Nicholas, I've seen you read Tarot plenty of times and know how good you are at it. You have a way of seeing things in the cards that I miss. We've already talked about working on your other skills. Working here at the shop is the perfect opportunity for you to do so."

Nick fidgeted from side to side. "I don't know. You know how I am around new people."

She narrowed her eyebrows. "Why are you fighting me on this? You came in here asking for a job, and I'm offering you one."

He withdrew inside himself, his shoulders going concave. "I meant a job like sweeping or stacking the shelves."

"I don't need a janitor. I need a Tarot reader, a talented one like yourself."

Nick threw his hands up in the air. "But you know I'm inexperienced. I've never read for anyone but myself."

"Don't you think it's time to branch out then?"

"But not with real people!"

"Then with whom? Pretend people?"

They stared at each other for a long moment, and then both burst out laughing. "I understand, Nicholas, I really do. I was like you once—incredibly shy and terrified of being wrong or saying the wrong thing. But the only way to get over this is to dive right in." She rested her hand on his arm. "And I'll be right in the next room. You can always come and get me if things get too dicey."

Nick wrung his hands. Even thinking about it caused his heart to pound in his chest. Maybe he could give it a shot and see how it goes—if he can somehow manage to get past his terror, that is.

"I guess I could try it." A strange feeling of relief washed over him.

"Yay! I'm so glad. I could really use the help."

"I thought you said you could barely pay the bills as it is?"

"I said the *store* wasn't bringing in money. I'm busier than hell with readings. The problem is that I have to turn most people away. There's only one of me, and there are only so many hours in a day. With the two of us doing readings, we'll be able to help a lot more people."

"I can only work after school."

She grinned. "Of course. How about Saturdays?"

He shrugged. "Sure. I usually don't have too much going on. Sometimes, I have to help my dad around the house, but we could work around that."

"Great. So here's how this will work. I'll book readings for you, you do them here, and we split your fee. Is sixty-forty fair to you?"

"Sixty-forty?"

"You keep sixty percent, and I keep forty."

"I guess. But there's one thing I don't understand."

"And that is?"

"I thought you didn't want me to do any paranormal work."

She shook her head and brushed a tuft of red hair off of her face. "I don't want you out in the field crossing over ghosts. That's what seems to be attracting the attention of this shadow creature, or whatever in the hell it is. From what your friend said, it's targeting mediums. The work you'll be doing here is different. You won't have that direct line to The Other Side. Instead, you'll be relying on your innate psychic ability—your intuition. Understand?"

"I think so," Nick said.

"When I corresponded with your friend Nate, I asked him the exact same question. He seems to think it's safe for psychics. It's when a medium is trying to cross over a ghost that there are problems. That's usually when our unwelcome visitor makes an appearance."

"When do I start?"

"First, there's one condition of your employment. You have to get permission from your parents."

He was hoping he wouldn't have to tell his parents about losing his job—at least not right away. "Oh, come on. I can't do that. You know they'd never go for it."

"You're not giving them enough credit. I know it was rough going at first with them, but you have to admit that they're coming around. They've done nothing but support you in this."

He scowled but shrugged. "I guess you're right. I'll talk to them. But I wouldn't be too sure about them agreeing to let me do Tarot readings. That's pushing it."

"I had a nice talk with them the last time I was over at your house." She flashed him a look. "You remember that night Nicholas, don't you? The night when none of us knew where you were or whether you were alive or dead."

"I remember," he said in a quiet voice. Nick recalled that night only too well. It was the night he'd broken his promise to his parents and to Katrina to help a ghost and nearly got himself killed in the process.

"So while I visited with your mom and dad, I explained to them the importance of what you do and stressed the impact it has on the lives of others. Even though I know they were uncomfortable talking about it, their auras told me that they were immensely proud of you." She raised an eyebrow. "They might surprise you."

"I hope you're right. Either that or they'll think I've completely lost my mind."

She laughed. "That is also a possibility."

"Oh, I almost forgot to tell you. I'm going to the prom."

Katrina's mouth dropped open. "You're doing what?"

"Going to the prom."

She drummed her fingers on the counter. "I certainly didn't see this coming. With whom?"

"Her name's Ericka. She asked me today."

"She asked you? I thought the boy was supposed to ask the girl. Or am I just old-fashioned?"

"You're just old-fashioned."

She swatted at him, but he ducked. "Why don't I know anything about this girl Ericka?"

"Probably because I didn't know her at all until today."

"So she asked you out of the blue?"

Nick nodded. "She came up during lunchtime and asked if I'd take her."

She studied his face for a moment. "I see. And is Gabe going to this prom as well?"

Nick instinctively reared back. Why was she asking about Gabe? He hadn't told her about him. He hadn't told anyone. He finally nodded. "He's going with Ericka's friend, Tana."

"So the plot thickens." She narrowed her eyes. "Is there anything perchance that you'd like to tell me?"

"About the prom?"

She shook her head and smiled. "Not exactly. I'm not blind, you know."

She knows. "I'm not sure what you mean."

She rolled her eyes and sighed. "Fine. You don't have to tell me. We can talk when you're ready."

Nick took a deep breath. After everything she had done for him, it was wrong to hide this aspect of himself from her. Not that he could anyway, given that she was psychic. He'd been thinking more and more about coming out to his family. Doing it with Katrina might be a good person to start with. Plus he was pretty certain she already knew as she's hinted about it several times.

"Do you mean about Gabe and me?" he stammered, his voice cracking as he spoke. He felt the hotness rise in his cheeks.

She had a soft smile on her face. "Yes, that. I know Nicholas. It's okay."

He nodded. "It's all still kind of new for me. I had no idea that..." He paused, trying to find the right words. "that Gabe was like me, that he felt the same way I do. I just found out only a few weeks ago. So now we're kinda seeing each other."

"Only kind of?"

"No, we are...seeing each other, I mean. We're boyfriends."

She clapped enthusiastically. "That's marvelous! I like him. I can definitely see the two of you together." She rested her hands on the counter and intertwined her fingers. "So, are you going to tell me what the situation is with the prom? How does Gabe feel about you taking a female date to the dance?"

Nick told her about his earlier conversation with Ericka.

"Oh, so she's going to be your beard."

"My what?"

She laughed. "Back in the old days, the term 'beard' referred to someone of the opposite sex that accompanied a gay man or woman to a social event, especially if said gay person was still in the closet. I suppose you could think of it as a sham date." She creased her brow. "You don't hear the term too often these days. I suppose because more people are open about their sexuality now than they were in the past."

Nick felt himself blush again. He wasn't used to talking about this kind of thing with anyone except Gabe. Especially an adult. Thinking of himself as gay was also going to take a bit of getting used to.

"It's kind of cool that Gabe and I get to go to the prom together. Well, not really together, but together."

"I've heard of same-sex couples going to the prom at some high schools, although it does tend to create a tad of an uproar. But it is becoming more and more acceptable these days. Now, if you and Gabe were really brave—"

"No way. Having a beard works just fine for me. I'm not ready for the entire world to know about me. Maybe when I'm like forty."

She laughed. "I have a feeling that you'll come out a lot sooner than that. Look how easy it was to talk to me about it."

He nodded. "But it's easy to talk to you about anything."

CHAPTER TWO

As Nick entered the main hall at Itona High, he was stunned by the intensity of the colors—mainly blue, white, and silver. The theme for the prom was "The Frozen Formal," based on Disney's popular film, *Frozen*. Everything in the room was of various shades of blue: the tablecloths, the curtains that draped the walls, even the lights were blue. Attached to the back of each chair was a group of six round balloons, three blue and three silver, with an imprinted bright white snowflake on each balloon. From the ceiling hung large white glittering snowflakes on a silver string, which some of the taller kids had to duck underneath as they maneuvered across the room.

At the center of the buffet table stood a towering ice castle sculpture, bathed in blue and white lights that gave it an otherworldly shimmer. A frozen river of dark blue wound its way around the edges of the table in sharp, deliberate zigzags, like a miniature moat keeping the icy fortress safe. Everything on the buffet table glowed in shades of blue —cool, majestic, and a little dramatic.

In contrast, the beverage table sparkled in white and

silver, like the glittery aftermath of a snowstorm. There were silver-rimmed paper plates printed with a white castle, translucent plastic cups with a metallic sheen, and snowflake-shaped napkins as crisp and delicate as the real thing. A gleaming white glass punch bowl took center stage, wrapped in a string of tiny blinking white lights that gave it the air of something enchanted.

Hovering above it all was a giant poster of Elsa and Anna, eyes wide and hopeful, arms flung open like they were inviting everyone to sing along. Nick had never seen *Frozen*, but thanks to his sister's nonstop commentary over the years about the film, he knew more about the two sisters than he'd ever asked for.

A generously sized dance floor stretched across the center of the room, tiled in alternating blue and white squares like some kind of winter-themed chessboard. Hovering above it, suspended from the ceiling, was a giant dark blue sign with bold white letters that read: *Frozen Formal*. It swayed ever so slightly, as if caught in an invisible breeze.

Nick had to admit—he was impressed. The decorations were elaborate, detailed, and honestly kind of magical. Clearly, the prom committee hadn't just slapped this together. Someone had poured time, effort, and probably an unhealthy obsession with *Frozen* into making this place look like a high schooler's version of Arendelle.

Nick's eyes roamed around the room. Who knew that high school kids could look so good? The dresses that the girls wore were stunning, many of them bordering on the outrageous. Nick's date, Ericka, wore a strapless dark pink dress that hugged her tight body, showing off all of her curves. It flowed outward at the floor, and in the middle of her back, the dress formed into a giant bow. Her hair, which was brushed to the rear the last time he'd seen her, now sat on top of her head, held up by a sizable sparkly pin. If only the guys at Gallowspine High could see him now, escorting one of the hottest girls in school to the prom. Of course, Nick had the hottest boy in school as his actual prom date.

Contrary to Nick's black tux and dark purple tie, Gabe wore a white tux and a black bow tie, the tux matching Tana's dress, which was also white with embroidered dark white lace. She had dark hair, much longer than Ericka's, that curled behind her ears and then down her shoulders and intense chocolate brown eyes. Tana was also shorter than Ericka by at least four inches and not quite as thin. She also had a slight roughness about her that made the dress seem a bit out of character for her. Nick guessed that she would be more at home wearing blue jeans than a fancy prom dress.

Nick and Gabe each had a dark yellow flower pinned to their tuxes, which they'd purchased for each other, while the girls had exchanged light blue wrist corsages. They stood at the railing watching the kids dance.

"Did you want to dance?" Nick asked Ericka. She was wearing a perfume that smelled like jasmine. Nick liked it.

She deadpanned him and then winked. "Not with you."

"Good. I'm not much of a dancer."

Gabe, who was standing next to Nick, leaned into Nick's arm. "I'll dance with you," he said into Nick's ear.

"You want to get us killed?" Nick said.

"I don't think they'd kill us," Gabe said. There was a crooked smile on his face. "Perhaps run us out of the building with torches, but not kill us. But then again..."

Nick gave him a smirk. "So, what do you think about this prom business?"

"I'm glad we came," said Gabe. "The band is decent,

and dinner out was fun. I'd never had Spiedini until tonight. Yum!"

"Isn't it great? I discovered it last year during Christmas when a friend of my mom's brought some over. Now I order it every chance I get."

"I think it's my new favorite food, too," Gabe said. "I'm so glad you suggested I try it." He pointed to Nick's empty glass. "More punch?"

"My turn to go," said Nick. "You went last time." He held up his glass. "Ladies? More punch?"

They both shook their head in unison. Nick grabbed his and Gabe's cup and navigated his way towards the punch bowl. Nick's head swam from the clash of the various waves of perfumes and colognes that hit him. He seemed to have become more sensitive to smells lately, especially when there were so many different ones in the same room.

He got about halfway to the beverage table when his stomach flip-flopped, and goosebumps rose on his skin. The intense feeling caught him so off-guard that he had to steady himself against the wall. There was a ghost nearby. Funny, he hadn't noticed any spirit activity until now.

He slowly turned his head so as not to attract any undue attention. He couldn't pinpoint anyone specifically who could be a ghost. Then, a couple moved out of the way, and Nick saw him. The only reason Nick was sure this was the spirit in question was because of the way he was dressed. Considering every other guy in the room was wearing a tux, the kid's dark blue short-sleeved work shirt and matching pants definitely stood out. The top two buttons of his shirt were undone, revealing a smooth, bare chest. Instead of dress shoes, he wore scuffed light brown construction boots, and a red bandana dangled casually from his front pocket. His short-cropped black hair contrasted sharply with his pale skin, giving him an almost ghostly kind of intensity. He was tall and lean, every line of his body well-proportioned and effortless. From where Nick was standing, the guy looked—well, annoyingly handsome. A girl carrying two drinks turned the corner and walked right through him. Yup, this guy was definitely a ghost.

Nick noticed that the spirit was gazing fixedly at someone near the punch bowl. Nick moved in closer in order to get a better look. He was staring at a kid with curly blond hair which fell in ringlets on his head, who was talking with a pretty blond girl in a dark green gown.

Nick shuffled closer, pretending to look at his phone. He now stood only about four feet away from the spirit. His skin was flawless, and he had brilliant green eyes, the color of chartreuse. His face looked tense as he watched the couple, almost in a scowl. The girl walked away, and the curly-haired blond kid stood stiffly and then looked around the room as though searching for an escape route. The ghost was watching every move the boy made. Nick could feel waves of anger coming from the spirit, and he wondered if the ghost meant the boy harm.

Unable to help himself, he stared at the spirit, wondering what he would do next. Nick didn't often see ghosts around his own age. Now that he thought about it, he couldn't remember ever seeing a ghost his age. The last one had been a soldier, only a few years older than Nick when he'd died.

The handsome ghost must have sensed that Nick was staring, because he turned his head and met Nick's gaze. Nick nonchalantly looked away.

"What in the hell are you looking at, pretty boy?"

Despite himself, Nick chuckled. He turned to meet the ghost's gaze again, momentarily forgetting his promise about not talking to spirits. "Really? Me? Pretty boy? You're kidding, right?"

The ghost whirled to face him. He widened his eyes, and every vestige of color drained from his already pale face. "You can see me?"

Oh shit. Katrina is going to be so pissed. "Yeah, I can see you."

"How?"

Nick shrugged. "Just one of the lucky ones, I guess." It seemed like such a lame thing to say, but he had nothing else. "So why are you here?"

The kid's demeanor changed. "Why in the fuck do you want to know?"

"Hey, I'm just asking," said Nick. "No need to be so rude. Trying to be friendly, that's all."

"Either way, it's none of your business."

Nick pressed further. "So why are you gaping at that curly-haired kid over there? Do you know him or something?"

All at once, Nick felt a powerful blast of chilly air that sent him reeling back. The ghost now stood only inches away from his face. Fury raced out of him, and his expression morphed into one of absolute rage. "Mind your own business!"

Nick flinched. "I was just asking—"

"And stay away from him!"

With that, the ghost disappeared. After a stunned moment, Nick looked around and breathed a sigh of relief. Luckily, nobody had noticed him talking to the spirit. By the time he approached the punchbowl, the blond kid was also gone.

With trembling hands, Nick refilled the red punch cups with a greenish liquid that didn't look all that appealing. He glanced around the room, but there was no sign of the ghost. The blond kid sat at a tiny table with another couple. One look at his face told Nick this guy was definitely not having fun. Nick then noticed Gabe, who was now standing by himself.

"Where are the girls?" Nick asked, handing Gabe his cup. Gabe flashed him a nuclear smile that shot straight to his heart.

"Said they wanted to take a stroll. I'm thinking they just wanted to go somewhere to make out."

Nick laughed. "If so, I hope they don't get caught. It might get awkward for us if our dates got busted kissing each other."

"If that happens, we'll just claim ignorance and act utterly shocked and appalled at their unseemly behavior. And speaking of behavior, where did you get off to? You were gone for an awfully long time."

Nick moved in closer to Gabe's ear. Gabe's soft blond hair gently stroked Nick's cheek. "There was a ghost incident."

Gabe's eyes grew wide. "You saw a ghost? Here?"

"Uh-huh. A guy who looked to be about our age. He was glaring at some kid." Nick scanned the room until he spotted the curly-haired boy now leaning against the wall on the other side of the room. He pointed him out. "Him. He's connected to the ghost somehow."

"Did you talk to the ghost?"

"He more or less shouted at me. He told me to mind my own frickin' business and leave blondie over there alone. He was pretty much a dick the entire time I talked to him. Totally batshit."

"Don't they usually want help or something?"

Nick shook his head. "Not this one. He wasn't at all

friendly and acted mighty pissed off that I could see him. He was kind of creepy."

"Is he still here?"

"Uh-uh. He disappeared when he finished screaming at me."

"Who disappeared?" ask Ericka. Nick hadn't even noticed that the girls had come back.

"Who's the kid with the blond curly hair?" Nick asked, ignoring her question. He pointed across the room.

"That's Tyler Tarrant," said Tana. "He's a little cutie, isn't he? Maybe *he'll* dance with me." Ericka jabbed her in the ribs with her elbow.

"Hey, I was just saying," said Tana. "No need to get all violent on me."

"I'll dance with you," said Ericka. She turned to look at Nick. "Why are you asking about Tyler? You know him or something? Or do you have a crush on him?"

"As if," said Nick. "No, I accidentally bumped into him on my way back. He doesn't seem to be having a very good time, does he?"

"It's sad about Tyler," said Tana, shaking her head. She lowered her voice. "Not many people know this, but he's gay as well. He came to the GSA a couple of times and even showed up once with his boyfriend. But about a year ago, his boyfriend died.

Nick feigned surprise. "Oh no. What happened? How did he die?

"I don't know any of the details of his death and didn't know him at all. I only met him once. He went to our school but was a year or two older than me. All I know is that Tyler hasn't been the same since then. Last year, he confided in me and told me what had happened. He was pretty wrecked by the whole thing. Tyler used to be a chatty guy who'd talk your ear off, but that all changed since his boyfriend's death. I have him in my Calc class now, and it's amazing how different he is. There aren't many of us who know what really happened and why he's so depressed these days. I hope he comes out of it."

"Do you know anything about his boyfriend?" asked Nick. "Like his name?"

"You mean the one who died?" said Tana.

Nick nodded.

"Not really. I don't remember if he even introduced himself when they came to the GSA meeting. He was pretty quiet." She narrowed her eyes. "Why all the questions?"

Nick swallowed, putting forth his best poker face. "Tyler looks familiar to me, and I wonder if I might have known his boyfriend. But I can't think of his name offhand or where I might know him from. Would you mind asking around to see if you can find out?"

"Sure, I guess," said Tana. "I'll ask some of the kids that were in our group. Maybe one of them remembers. I wouldn't feel comfortable asking Tyler himself." She turned to Gabe and pointed at him. "And you...it's time to fulfill your promise. You're going to dance with me."

Gabe raised his eyebrows and looked at Nick. Nick smiled. "Knock yourselves out."

Nick looked across the room for Tyler and saw him sitting alone at the same table he was at earlier—and the ghost was standing right next to him.

∽

"YOU GOT FIRED FROM YOUR JOB?" his father said, shaking his head. "For what reason?"

Nick cringed, feeling small under the disapproving stare of his parents. He dropped his gaze. "Attendance. Remember when I was helping the ghost, Mrs. Burton, who was murdered? And then the soldier?"

His father nodded his head and looked at Nick's mother. She had a stony expression on her face.

"I ended up missing a few days of work because of that," Nick said. "I wasn't aware that jobs through the Community Action Agency had a strict attendance policy. I guess I neglected to read the fine print."

"It shouldn't matter whether or not there is an attendance policy in place," said his father. "When you accept employment somewhere, you are inadvertently signing a contract saying that you will show up to work when scheduled. No employer allows their employees to come and go willy-nilly."

"Sorry, Dad."

"Don't tell me you're sorry. It's not me who you inconvenienced because you didn't hold up your end of the agreement. You should be apologizing to yourself, because in the long run, you're the one who's getting hurt. You not only failed the school, but you failed yourself. Getting fired from a job becomes part of your permanent employment record, making it more difficult to obtain a decent job in the future. Is that what you want?"

His words hit harder than any slap could have. "Of course not. I didn't think about it at the time. All I thought about was helping those people who needed me."

His father stared at him in silence, as though he didn't know what to say. After a couple of moments, his mother broke the silence. "That's commendable, Nick. I get that you want to help these..." she cleared her throat, "people. But that doesn't justify throwing away a perfectly good job.

You're going to have to learn to be more discerning about what you can and can't do. If you want spending money, you'll need a job—and that entails going to work when scheduled."

"I think I may have another job lined up," Nick said in a casual voice. Or at least that's what he was aiming for.

His father raised his eyebrows. "Already? Doing what?"

"Katrina offered me a position at her store."

His mother frowned. "At that spook shop?"

Nick nodded. "It's a New Age store. The job would be after school and on Saturdays."

His father raised an eyebrow. "What kind of work would you be doing exactly? Working behind the counter?"

"Not exactly." Nick swallowed and took a deep breath. "I'd be doing Tarot readings."

His mother gasped and looked at him sharply. He saw her shiver. "You mean like fortune-telling?"

"Kinda," Nick said, running a hand through his hair. "Katrina says I'm pretty good at it, and she could use the extra help at the shop. She says she's been turning away a lot of people because she doesn't have the time to serve everyone."

His mother snapped her head to look at his father. "John...."

His father folded his arms in front of his chest. "Aren't there any more respectable jobs you could get? Have you tried the grocery? They always seem to have job ads posted. Or maybe the gas station at the corner?"

"I have no interest in working at a grocery store or a gas station. I know Katrina, and it makes perfect sense for me to work there. She is, after all, giving me lessons."

His father met his gaze. "I don't know if I feel comfortable with my son being a fortune teller."

"I'm not going to be telling fortunes," Nick said. "The cards can help people make decisions when they're confused or don't know where else to turn. I know they've helped me out many times. They're more like a brain-storming tool. Many people use them to bring clarity to a confusing situation."

His parents looked at each other in silence. Nick continued. "And Katrina will be right there if I need any help or if there's a question that I can't answer."

"I don't know how people are going to feel going to a high school kid for advice," his father said. "You're only sixteen, after all."

"Almost seventeen," Nick corrected. "And ghosts and their families are already coming to me. They find me at school. They find me here. They find me in coffee shops. What's the difference if they find me at Katrina's shop?"

"Your mother and I will talk it over, and we'll let you know what we decide." His father's face softened. "This is something outside of our comfort zone. We're still trying to get used to the idea that our son is..." His father creased his brow, apparently trying to search for the right word.

"Psychic," Nick said, his voice sharper than he'd intended. "Actually, I'm a psychic medium. That's a psychic who can see spirits."

"Of course," said his father. He ran his fingers through his hair. "Give your mother and I some time to discuss it, and we'll get back to you."

As Nick walked up the stairs to his room he sighed, knowing that there wasn't a chance in hell his mom and dad would ever allow him to do Tarot readings. Not in a million years. He'd have to break the news to Katrina—and then go out job hunting. Perhaps there was a future for him bagging groceries after all.

CHAPTER THREE

NICK SAT PROPPED up in bed, with a small paperback copy of *The Catcher in the Rye* resting against his raised knees. He had twenty-eight more pages to read, and then he'd be caught up on his Lit class homework. They'd recently read *Lord of the Flies,* which Nick didn't enjoy as much as this book. There was something about Holden's character that resonated with Nick. Maybe the feeling of being an outcast?

His phone buzzed on his dresser. Nick picked it up and stared at the screen. It was a number he didn't recognize.

"Yeah?"

"Is this Nick?" a female voice at the other end said. What girl would be calling him?

"Yes, who's this?"

"Tana. Remember me? We went to the prom together."

Nick laughed. "Of course I remember you. I'm glad we did that. I had a lot of fun."

"Me too," she said. "You and Gabe make a good pair. He's a sweetie."

"That he is."

"So you asked me about Tyler Tarrant? I questioned a

couple of people at school who know Tyler, and supposedly, his boyfriend was nineteen and named Tony. I don't know his last name. According to one of Tyler's gay friends, Tony was out swimming by himself at Doctor's Park and drowned."

"That's rough," said Nick. "Nobody else was around?"

"Uh-uh. Some guy walking his dog noticed the body washed up on shore."

Nick shuddered. "Creepy. I hope I never stumble across a dead body.

"Right? I can't say as though I disagree with you on that," Tana said. "I don't even like coming across dead animals."

"And this was last year when Tony died?"

"I think so. That's when Tyler told me about it. A friend of mine who also had Tyler in a couple of her classes said that he took it pretty bad. He dropped out of the photography club, quit track, and from what she said, he hardly talks to anyone anymore."

"So he's still not over it, huh?

"Doesn't sound like it. Not many people in school know he's gay, so nobody has any idea what he's dealing with. I don't think he was out to his parents. Or at least he wasn't when he came to the GSA meeting if I remember correctly."

"What is he, a junior?"

"Senior. He graduates in May. That is if he's not flunking everything."

"This boyfriend of his, Tony. You mentioned he went to your school?"

"He did, but I don't think he finished. Given that he was older, I didn't know him at all. I do remember that he was wearing some sort of uniform when he came to the

GSA meeting that made me think he was something like an auto mechanic."

Nick recalled that the ghost was wearing something similar at the prom. It's funny. According to all the movies he's ever seen about ghosts, a ghost always wears the same outfit that they had on when they died. That's not been Nick's experience at all. From what he could tell, ghosts show up wearing the clothes that best fit their personality. If this Tony did drown in the lake while swimming, it was unlikely he was wearing his work uniform when it happened.

"Thanks, Tana. That's really helpful."

"No problem. Maybe the four of us can hang out together sometime?"

"Definitely," Nick said. "That'd be great. You guys are fun."

They said their goodbyes and promised they'd contact each other soon. Nick was now positive that the ghost who'd been hanging around Tyler was his dead boyfriend, Tony. So why was he still here? And why was he attached to Tyler? His uncle had told him that ghosts typically stayed around only when they had unfinished business of some kind. Did Tony really die in an accident, or was there more to it? Maybe he was murdered, and Tyler had something to do with it. The ghost had undoubtedly looked mighty pissed-off at the prom.

Nick laid down his book, jumped off the bed with a loud thump and padded to his computer. He did a Web search for "Doctors Park drowning'. Several results popped up right away. One entitled 'Local Boy Drowns at Doctors Park' caught his eye, and he clicked it. According to the post, the kid's name was Anthony Fisher, and he drowned while swimming by himself. An autopsy confirmed that the boy had indeed died by drowning. So he wasn't murdered—at least not according to the official report—and now Nick knew the ghost's last name. The other articles that came up pretty much said the same thing: a teen boy swimming by himself drowns in the lake. Nick groaned. None of this told him anything.

He was considering doing a Tarot reading about the situation to see if the cards could point him in the right direction when his mother's voice called him from downstairs. He closed the web browser, scooped up his jeans from the floor, and threw on an orange T-shirt—the one everyone said he looked good in. He thrust his phone into his back pocket and checked himself in the mirror. His mother's voice came again.

"I'm coming!" he said and darted down the stairs. The kitchen smelled faintly of burnt bacon.

"I thought you were never going to get up," his mother said. She was leaning against the counter with the daily newspaper spread out in front of her. She folded it closed.

"What do you mean? It's Saturday. There's no school today."

"That's no excuse for wasting away an entire day." She turned. "Do you want some breakfast? I can whip you up a cheesy omelet."

"That'd be great. And I wasn't wasting the day, by the way. I was reading a book for school."

"That's nice." She stood at the stove, watching the omelet with her back toward Nick. "Your father and I talked about what we discussed last night," she said without looking at him.

"About working with Katrina?" Nick asked.

"Yes," she said, her back still toward Nick. She reached

to the overhead cupboard and retrieved a plate. "Could you push the toast down for me?

Two slices of light brown rye bread stood in the toaster. Nick got up and pushed down the toaster handle. "So?"

"We decided that if you were going to work somewhere, it might as well be with your friend. It makes the most sense given that you're already studying with her a couple of times a week."

"Yes!" Nick said, fist-pumping the air.

His mother turned around and wiped her hands on her apron. "But there are a couple of conditions."

"Uh-oh. What kind of conditions?"

"If you run into anything frightening or morally ques- tionable, you need to promise me that you'll stop whatever it is you're doing and tell Katrina right away. And you are not to meet with strangers unless she is there in the store with you. Is that understood?"

Nick nodded. "Will do. I think there's some form that Katrina needs you to fill out for the government since I'm under eighteen—a work permit or something."

"Put it on the counter, and I'll sign it."

Nick got up from the table, retrieved the form from his backpack and placed it on the counter on top of his mother's newspaper. "Here."

She turned around for a moment and nodded. "By the way, who were you talking to upstairs?"

"Tana."

His mother scooped his omelet onto the plate. "I don't think you've mentioned her before."

"She was Gabe's prom date."

"Ah yes, the prom. You haven't talked about it much." Nick thought it was strange how she was staring at him so intently. "How was the prom?"

Nick shrugged. "Prom-like. Not too exciting."

"That girl you took—"

"Ericka."

"Yes, Ericka. Do you plan on seeing her again?"

"I see her every day at school."

"What I mean is do you plan on going out with her again?" she paused and swallowed. "Romantically."

Nick looked away. "No way, Mom. She's a friend. That's all."

"So, there's nothing more there?"

"Nope. She just needed someone to go to the prom with her, and being the gallant gentleman that I am, I offered to take her. That's it. Nothing more. No romance here."

She nodded and set the plate in front of him, topped with a fluffy yellow omelet. Melted white cheese oozed from the end of the omelet. "Eat your breakfast before it gets cold." She sat down across from Nick. "You'll tell us if you decide to date anyone, won't you?"

Nick put down his fork. He loathed these types of discussions. "I'm not planning on dating anyone."

"I imagine it wouldn't be easy telling a girlfriend about what you do. With the spirits, I mean."

"I suppose not," said Nick. This was an awfully strange conversation he was having. His parents never talked to him about dating or girls...or boys. He felt all kinds of uncomfortable. He wondered if a person could die from embarrassment.

She nodded and got up. "Put the plate in the sink when you're done. We'll talk some more later." She rose and left the room.

What in the hell was all that about? Nick hoped that she wasn't getting ready to have the birds and the bees talk with him. Please, anything but that.

~

"THAT'S MARVELOUS NEWS!" Katrina said. "Did you bring the signed work permit?"

Nick reached into the back pocket of his jeans. "Voila. Signed and dated, just like you asked."

She sighed. "You didn't have to scrunch it up in your pocket like that. This has to be sent to the state." She laid the form flat on her desk and dragged her hand across it, trying to smooth out the wrinkles. "That will have to do, I suppose. Let's hope they don't send it back."

"Sorry," he said. "I still can't believe my folks agreed to this. I never thought they'd sign it in a million years. They weren't happy about it at first, but they gave in. I wonder why?"

"I think it helped that they met me and now know who I am. They discovered I was a normal person, just like them."

"Ha Ha!" Nick said. "You're about as far away from normal as you can get."

"Now, Nicholas, don't make me hire you and fire you on the same day."

Nick crossed his arms over his chest. "You can't fire someone who hasn't even started yet."

She swatted at a large black fly that was buzzing around their heads but missed. "You can be maddening at times, much like this fly," she said, following the insect with her eyes. She turned her gaze back to Nick. "Perhaps it was not wise of me to bring such an irritating young man on board as a reader."

Nick shook his head. "You can't change your mind now. You promised me a job."

She gave him a broad smile. "I am kidding with you. So when can you start?"

He shrugged. "Anytime, I guess."

"How about this afternoon?"

"What? Already?"

She picked up the large appointment book off of her cluttered desk and flipped the pages. "I have a woman coming in for a reading. She's a new client, so I know nothing about her."

The snake of fear coiled in his stomach. He closed his eyes and pictured himself in a tiny dark room seated at a table with a stranger across from him. His heart sped up. "I didn't think I'd be doing this so soon. I haven't prepared at all."

She creased her brow, and her gaze lingered, looking at him curiously. "Exactly how did you intend to prepare?"

He took a deep breath and swallowed the sudden dryness in his throat. He groaned. "I dunno. Maybe review my Tarot card binder. Maybe read a Tarot book. Maybe—"

She took his hand, silencing him. "You can read the cards better already than many professional psychics who've been doing this for years. We've already had this talk. You are once again allowing self-doubt to seep in. This only causes you to shut down, and then where will you be?"

Nick felt some of the tension ease from his body. "You're right. I'll simply go with the flow. And if I screw it up, you're in the next room. You'd come in to rescue me, wouldn't you?"

She chuckled and shook her head. "You are not going to screw it up. Have some faith in yourself."

"I'll try. So, what time is the lady coming in?"

"Her name is Faith, and she'll be here in about," she paused and looked up at the clock. "Twenty minutes."

Nick's eyes grew wide. "That soon? Shit."

"Now, is that any kind of attitude? You should be excited about your first client."

He heaved a sigh. "I'm too nervous to be excited."

"You'll be fine. You can use my deck if you like. It's sitting on the window sill."

"No need," he said, shaking his head. "I brought my own."

She widened her eyes. "But how did you know you'd be reading today?"

"I didn't. I always stuff it in my backpack when I leave the house just in case I have a question that needs answering."

She smiled. "I'm glad to see that you're using the cards. Of course, you don't want to become too dependent on them."

"Of course."

She narrowed her eyes. "Are you mocking me, young man?"

He chuckled and said nothing.

"I'm serious about this, Nicholas. You mustn't consult the cards for every little thing. I've met some people who become so dependent on them that they cannot make even the tiniest decision without reading on it first. You never want to give your power away to anyone or anything."

"How do I know if I'm reading too much?"

"That's a difficult call. I personally only throw down the cards if I'm contemplating a major decision and want to look at it from a couple of different perspectives. Let's say that I'm torn between two job offers, one in Chicago and the other in Minneapolis. I might toss a few cards to see what the potential outcome might be if I went to Chicago, went to Minneapolis or stayed here. This would give me an idea of what might be in store for me, but ultimately, the decision is mine."

Nick nodded. "Understood. I'll be sure not to overdo it." He settled into his seat. "By the way, Gabe wants me to teach him how to read the cards. Do you think I should?"

"That's wonderful!"

"No, it's not. I mean, I'm just learning myself. I'm certainly not ready to teach anyone else. I wish he hadn't asked...and I wish I hadn't said yes."

"You're looking at this the wrong way. I have found that the best way of learning something—really learning it well— is to teach it. By teaching it to others, the concepts become even more ingrained in your brain and force you to truly focus. I think that by teaching your boyfriend, you'll become a better card reader in the process."

Boyfriend. It was the first time that anyone besides Tana and Ericka referred to Gabe as his boyfriend, and it warmed his heart. "I'll give it a shot. Who knows? Maybe he'll end up being a better card reader than me."

She laughed. "Anything is possible, Nicholas." She glanced at her wristwatch, which was on a wide white watchband that looked ridiculously large on her tiny wrist. She must have an entire collection of those bands because every time Nick saw her, she wore the same style of watchband, only in a different color. Maybe he'll buy her a skinny watchband for Christmas. "We have a few minutes. Let's discuss the proper way to do a reading for another person. You remember the method of asking questions of the cards, correct?"

Nick nodded. "No questions containing the word 'should' and no yes/no questions. And no psychic snooping."

Katrina quirked a smile at him. "Wherever did you hear that term from?"

"My uncle cautioned me about it once. He said that I shouldn't allow anyone to ask a question about someone else unless I have that person's permission. I think he called it a third-party reading. If I'm not mistaken, I believe you told me about it as well during one of your lessons."

"Very good. These same rules apply to the client. Try to rephrase their question if need be so that the reading empowers them. Remember—your client should always be in a better place when they leave you than they were when they came." She brushed back a strand of hair with her hand. "So, what's the first thing you say to a client."

"Hello?"

She heaved an exasperated sigh. "After that."

Nick thought about it for a moment. "What's your question?"

"You need to listen, Nicholas. My question was..."

"No, I meant that's what I'd ask the client. I'd say, 'What's your question?'"

"You might want to soften it a bit. I usually begin by asking them something along the lines of, 'so what brings you to see me today?' as a way to break the ice. It also gives me an idea of what kind of information they're interested in. But often, clients don't have a specific question and prefer a general type of reading."

"How in the hell can you read the cards if there's no question?"

"I determine ahead of time how many cards to lay down. I might throw down six or nine cards and then let the pictures tell me the story. The client is often amazed at how much information comes through."

"I don't think I'd like that very much at all. I prefer to know what I'm asking about."

"You'll need to learn how to do it both ways. A good reader can adapt to any situation or any client."

Nick rubbed his forehead with his palm and shut his eyes. "This is a lot more complicated than I thought it'd be."

"Not really," said Katrina. "A lot of this comes down to experience. The longer you do this, the more you'll be prepared for the different types of readings people will ask you to do."

"What if I don't know the answer?"

"You read the cards to the best of your ability, and recount what you see to the client. There are times, however, when you simply cannot make a connection. It happens to all of us."

"So, what do you do in those circumstances?"

"Cheerfully refund their money."

"What if that happens to me today?"

"Oh, ye of little faith," Katrina said, smiling. "If your nerves get in the way, I'll take over. I'm right in the next room."

Nick opened his mouth to ask another question when the bell above the door rang. Two women who looked to be in their 40's entered.

"Can I help you?" asked Katrina.

Nick's stomach somersaulted, and gooseflesh rose on his skin. He stared at the two women, and his heart began to race.

"My name's Faith. I have an appointment for a reading."

"Ah yes, I have you here," said Katrina. She looked at the other woman. "But we only allow one person at a time in the reading room."

"That's fine," said Faith. "There's only me here."

Katrina creased her brow and looked at the other woman. She was just about to speak when Nick gently kicked her shin. She snapped her head toward Nick. He mouthed the word "ghost." Her face drained of color. She quickly held out a clipboard and asked Faith to please sign the consent form.

"You both can see me, can't you!" the other woman exclaimed.

Faith was in the midst of reading the form. Nick faced the other woman, and he held up an index finger to his mouth. The woman reared back, a confused look on her face.

"Nicholas here will conduct your reading today," said Katrina.

The disappointment was clear on Faith's face. "Oh, I understood you would be doing the reading."

"We have more than one reader here at the shop," Katrina said. She gave Nick a half-smile and turned back to Faith. "Believe me when I tell you that Nick here is the perfect reader for you."

She nodded. "I suppose it's alright."

Katrina gestured to the back room with her head.

"Oh, right," Nick said. "If you'd like to follow me."

"Don't forget your deck, Nick."

"I don't think—" he began.

"Here, this one is handy," Katrina said, handing him her deck. She mouthed, "take it," and he did.

Once in the back, Faith took the chair across from Nick. The other woman stood in the corner, watching. "So, what brings you in to see me today?"

"My sister," said Faith.

"That's me!" said the other woman.

"She's deceased, I take it?"

Faith studied his face for a moment before answering and then nodded. "You *are* good. Yes, she died about four months ago."

"What was her name?" asked Nick.

"Stephanie," both women said in unison. Nick bit his bottom lip in order to prevent himself from laughing.

"Tell her I'm still here," said Stephanie. "You have to let her know that I'm sorry!"

Nick looked up for a moment, raised his eyebrows as Stephanie, and then returned his regard back to Faith. "What do you need to know?"

"I need to know if Steph is still angry with me—and whether she's at peace."

Nick nodded, snatched up his deck, and began shuffling. He laid out four cards on the table.

"Tell her I'm sorry I was angry about those stupid dishes. It was wrong of me."

Nick stared at the cards but didn't really see them. "There was a disagreement about some dishes?"

"My mother's dishes," said the ghost. "She got them when Mama died, and I was so mad that I didn't talk to her for fourteen years."

"They were your mother's dishes," added Nick. "And she was angry that you got them and not her."

Faith gasped and brought her hand up to her mouth. "Oh, my god. It's true. We didn't talk for many years because of it. I took the dishes from my mother's house. Steph said that Mama had promised them to her, but I took them anyway." She looked down at the table. Nick could see the embarrassment on her face. "We stopped speaking to each other—all because of those dishes."

"Fourteen years, right?" asked Nick.

She glanced back up at him, her eyes open wide. She looked stunned. "It was exactly fourteen years. In fact, we never talked again. I never got to see her before she passed. I never got a chance to apologize."

"She forgives you," said Nick. "And she says she's sorry."

"Tell her that because of my stubbornness, I never got a chance to know my two nephews."

"You see all of that in the cards?" Faith asked.

Okay, time to come clean. "The cards just helped me to make the connection. I have your sister here now."

"Steph is here? Like, right here in this room?"

Nick nodded. "You have two kids, both boys?"

Faith nodded but said nothing. Nick continued. "She regrets that she didn't have a chance to get to know her two nephews."

"Tell her I was young and pigheaded at the time," said the ghost. "It was only right that she got the dishes. I was still angry at Mama for giving Faith her jewelry box before she died."

Nick creased his brow. "Your mother gave you a jewelry box before she died?"

"Yes. When my mama was sick—she died from cancer—she gave me her jewelry box with all the jewelry. Not that she had a lot. Why?"

"She said that back then, she thought it was unfair that you got both the dishes and the jewelry box."

"But she got the damned house!"

Nick looked at Stephanie. She nodded. "I was horribly greedy and immature when I was younger," said Stephanie. "I didn't mind the jewelry box so much. But it was the principle of the thing. When Mama found out that I was pregnant, she promised me the dishes for our new home. The dishes were supposed to go to me."

"She's still kinda pissed about the dishes."

"I am not!" said Stephanie.

"You are too," said Nick. "You're supposed to be making amends here."

She glowered at him. "You are certainly smart-mouthed for a teenager."

Nick laughed, despite his determination to remain professional.

"Are you talking to her?" asked Faith.

"Sorry," Nick said. "I forgot you can't see her." He took a deep breath. "So, if I've got this right, your mother promised her the dishes when she found out Stephanie was pregnant. But instead of her getting them, you took them?"

Faith nodded. "I was young and greedy at the time."

"She said almost exactly the same thing about herself," said Nick. He picked up the cards off the table without thinking and began shuffling. "Basically, this thing boils down to *stuff*, right?"

Steph looked at him and nodded. "Once you put it that way, yes. I supposed that's true."

Faith pursed her lips. "When you phrase it like that, it all sounds so trivial." She looked up. "Oh Steph, honey, I'm so sorry that I let this come between us. It was stupid and wrong of me."

The ghost nodded and dabbed at her eyes. "Tell her I'm sorry, too. Oh, to think about all the years we wasted being angry about a jewelry box and dishes."

"She says she's sorry that she let the stuff come between you. She wished she hadn't wasted all of those years being angry."

"Me too," said Faith. She reached for the Kleenex box, pulled out a tissue, and blew her nose.

Without thinking, Nick turned over a card. It was The Star.

Faith's eyes drifted to the card. "What does that mean?"

"It's a card of forgiveness. It's time for you both to forgive each other so each of you can move on." Nick pointed to the giant yellow star in the center of the card. "See this? This represents the light—Stephanie's light. She needs to move on now to the next stage of her journey. Your disagreement was the only thing that's kept her from crossing over." Where this was all coming from, Nick had no idea.

"I forgive you," they both said at the same time. Tears streaked down Faith's face.

Nick heard Stephanie gasp and turned to look. She was pointing to the window. "Is that it? Is that the light?"

"It must be," said Nick.

"What's she saying?" asked Faith.

"She sees her light. It's time for her to leave."

"She's going? Now?"

"It's finally her time."

"Oh, my God. Goodbye, Stephanie! I love you."

"I love you, too," said Stephanie. She walked over and kissed Faith on the forehead. "Goodbye, Sis. I'll see you on the other side." With that, she disappeared.

Faith brought her hand up to the exact same place on her forehead where Stephanie had kissed her. She stared at Nick, wide-eyed.

He closed his eyes for a moment and nodded. "She's gone."

She grabbed a couple more tissues and dabbed at both

of her eyes. "I'm so sorry I ever doubted you, young man. You're really something else!"

Nick felt himself blush. "Thanks. I'm so glad you both were able to fix the rift between you."

"And I thank you for providing me with the opportunity to say goodbye to my sister. It means the world to me." She reached into her purse, pulled out a folded bill and handed it to Nick. "This is for you. You can count on me coming back."

She stood up, and Nick followed suit. She extended her hand. "You are quite the impressive young man. See you soon." She turned on her heel and left the room. Nick unfolded the note she gave him. It was a $100 bill.

Katrina smiled at him when he came back out in front. He handed her the bill.

"That's yours, Nicholas," she said.

"But I thought we split the income?"

"She already paid for her session. You get to keep whatever tips you make." Her eyes stared at the bill. "She gave you a hundred dollars?"

Nick nodded. "I didn't know it was a tip. I thought she was paying for the session."

"She obviously liked her reading," said Katrina. She propped her elbows on the counter and rested her head in her hands. "So, how did it go?"

Nick shrugged. "I didn't do much of anything. The ghost came in with her sister. All I had to do was spit back what she said."

Katrina shook her head and sighed. "Didn't do much of anything? Honestly, Nicholas. You are always underestimating your ability. I certainly couldn't have done that, given that I don't see ghosts unless I'm standing right next to you. Very few people can. She was the perfect client for you, and you were the perfect reader for her. Don't you see? I have always said that we receive the clients that we are meant to."

"I guess you're right. It was pretty easy-peasy."

"So since I didn't see the ghost come out with her sister, I assumed you crossed her over?"

Nick nodded. "The whole purpose of her visit was to—"

"Uh-uh," Katrina said, wagging her index finger at him. "Remember, confidentiality?"

"Even between us?"

She nodded. "The trust that's between a client and a reader is a sacred trust. What is discussed in that room stays in that room."

"Can I tell you one weird thing that happened?"

"As long as you don't divulge what was said."

"I was talking to Faith, the one who wasn't the ghost, and I didn't even realize that I had picked up the cards. The Star card came up, and these odd meanings for it just popped into my head out of nowhere. I knew that she was going to cross over today because of the bright star in the card. Weird, huh?"

"I think now you're beginning to understand how this all fits into place. That was your psychic ability at work. Sometimes, when I'm doing a reading, I don't remember a thing I said afterward. It's like I'm a channel."

Nick furrowed his brow. "A channel?"

"The words aren't coming from me but rather from an outside source."

"Like a ghost?" Nick asked.

"Could be. I've always thought about it as coming from spirit. Other people might think of it as coming from God, Goddess, a ghost, or their Higher Self. That's what psychic ability is—the power to obtain information that you normally wouldn't have access to."

"That's exactly the way it was. I had no idea where the words were coming from. But once they left my mouth, they made sense."

"I told you that you had nothing to fear." She laid a hand on Nick's shoulder and closed her eyes. "Ah yes, the Force is strong in this one."

Nick shrugged her hand off. "Ha-ha. Very funny."

She laughed. "All kidding aside, you now see how this works. You need to have faith that what is meant to come through, will."

"The reading was actually kind of fun," Nick said. "Both of them were nice ladies."

"Most of the clients that come here are nice. They come here for help and guidance. The skeptics and nonbelievers usually don't come to psychics."

Nick looked down at her appointment book. "Do I have any more today?"

"So eager you are all of a sudden!" she said, and chuckled. She glanced at her appointment book. "No, that's it for today. The rest are my regular clients."

He gestured to the book. "Why don't you have that on your computer? A paper planner is so last century. I could put it all in Outlook or Google Calendar for you."

"I prefer it the old-fashioned way, thank you very much. I don't have to worry about my paper book crashing, breaking or needing to be recharged—and I can take it with me wherever I go."

"I promise once you get the hang of it, you'd love it."

She shook her head. "You'll have to get used to my last-century ways of doing things. This girl's not gonna change. I like to keep things simple."

"Writing everything out by hand is what you call simple? Wouldn't you like to access your appointments from your phone?"

"Why on earth would I want to do that? The only time I need to see them is when I'm here at the shop." She pointed to the book. "And it's quick and easy access. I don't have to wait for it to boot up."

"Suit yourself," Nick said. "But if you change your mind, I'll be happy to fix you up."

"I won't be changing my mind, I assure you."

Nick smiled. "If you don't have any more appointments for me, then I'm gonna take off."

"Remember—no blabbing about your reading."

"Not even to Gabe?"

"To nobody. You can talk about the reading in general terms as long as you don't discuss any of the specifics. How would you like it if I went to your school and told everyone that you could see ghosts?"

"That wouldn't be very nice."

"No, it wouldn't. Nor would breaking the confidence of your client."

"Okay, I get it. I'll make sure that I never tell Gabe or anyone else anything specific that was said." He raised his eyebrows. "Can I tell him that I crossed a ghost over? He enjoys hearing about the ghost stuff."

She laughed. "That's fine, given that he's been helping you out." Her expression grew serious. "We still need to be prudent about not attracting the attention of whatever it is that's causing the disturbance on the Other Side. I'd still prefer it if you don't cross anyone else over except for when you're here."

"What's the difference if I cross 'em over here or somewhere else?"

"This is sacred space. I use herbs and rituals to protect this shop from any negative entities that might try and wander in." She frowned. A shadow crossed over her expression, and there was sudden doubt in her eyes. "Or at least I hope they're strong enough." She locked eyes with him. "Now that you mention it, I really don't know if it's enough, given that we don't know anything about this demon. Who knows if my protections will even work? You should probably try to minimize your contact with the Other Side as much as possible—that means no crossing ghosts over and no communicating with them, no matter where you are. Even here."

"It's difficult," said Nick. "To ignore the spirits, I mean. So many of them seem so desperate. It's sad."

"I know, honey. But you don't want to put yourself in any danger." She fiddled with the calendar on her desk for a moment and then turned her regard back to him. "Truth be told, I didn't even consider the possibility that you'd be dealing with a ghost today. It never once crossed my mind. The client said that she wanted a Tarot reading."

"It's not your fault. The lady had no idea that her sister was attached to her. She herself thought she was coming in for just a reading."

"You're right." She rubbed the back of her neck, and her expression darkened. "Maybe bringing you on at the shop wasn't such a good idea after all. The last thing I want to do is to put you in any danger."

"It's only a Tarot reading, like you said." *Except when ghosts decide to tag along*.

She nodded. "I'm hoping that today was an atypical situation." She held up her hand and crossed her fingers. "And I'm counting on my protections and wards being strong enough to shield any activity that goes on here."

"What's a ward? Is that what you meant by herbs and rituals?"

"Yes. A ward is kind of a protection spell. A friend of mine who's exceptionally good at that sort of thing did it for me awhile ago." She tapped her chin. "I wonder if I should have her redo them? Maybe reinforce them or add stronger ones?"

"A spell? Do you mean like witchcraft?"

"Yes, and..."

"Are you talking about witches? Real ones?"

"I am, but that's a topic for another day. But I will ensure that this shop is protected from negative energies and entities as much as humanly possible."

"That'd be a good thing. But please don't fire me already, okay?"

She smiled. "Of course you're not fired. You did really well today. But maybe next time, don't let the ghost know you can see it. At least until this blows over. I'll e-mail Nate later on. Hopefully, there have been some fresh developments."

"Last time I heard from him, he said that they're working on an idea. He wouldn't tell me any of the specifics, though."

"I don't blame him. They're probably trying to keep the entity in the dark about what they're planning." She gave him a stern look. "And you having such an open and strong connection to the Other Side doesn't help."

His heart sank. "Sorry. I'll be better."

She snickered. "It's not your fault at all. Just try not to cross over anyone else."

"I won't." He decided that now would not be the right time to tell her about Tony, the ghost at the prom. "I can still read Tarot, right?"

She sat back and pressed her index finger to her chin. "As long as it doesn't involve ghosts, I don't see why not."

"And it's okay to teach Tarot to someone else?"

She raised her eyes and stiffened. "You're planning on teaching Tarot? Already?"

"It's not like that. Gabe's been pestering me to teach him the cards, and I promised him I would—although I have been putting it off. I could at least show him what I know and let him play with a deck. I haven't even shown him my uncle's Tarot binder."

"Ah, yes—I'd forgotten you mentioned that," she said, breaking out into a grin. "I think that'd be good for you both." She paused. "I'm happy that Gabe is so accepting of your work. You're very fortunate in that aspect."

"I know. He's been fantastic. However, I'm still not sure how I feel about teaching him the cards. It's kinda weird."

"You don't have to be psychic to learn Tarot. Anyone can do it, and if you ask me, everyone's at least a little psychic. Most people just haven't learned how to tap into it. I think it's good that Gabe wants to learn the cards. It'll bring you even closer together. Maybe he'll find them helpful in his life as well."

"Hey, perhaps he can even get a job with you at the shop," Nick said. He flashed her his best mischievous grin.

"One of you is more than enough." She flicked her wrist in the air. "Now, off with you. Some of us have work to do."

CHAPTER FOUR

"HI DEAN, this is Nick Michelson. I'm not sure if you remember me, but..."

"Hell yes, I remember you! How could I ever forget the handsome man who saved my life?"

If Nick weren't on the phone, he would have blushed. "I didn't exactly save your life. You did that yourself, with the help of your dad."

"If you hadn't stepped in, I hate to think where I'd be right now."

"So, how's the new school?" Nick asked, eager to change the subject.

"Fantastic," Dean answered. "Nobody taunts me or bullies me here. It's nice being able to walk down the halls without having to watch my back constantly. My dad seems much happier too, since the move."

A wave of disappointment washed over Nick. "Did you move out of the area? You no longer live in Gallowspine Mountains?

"We moved but only twenty miles away to Ashnor. My stepdad wanted a completely new start for us, so he bought a house there, which is pretty awesome of him. For me, it feels like an entirely new life."

"That's great news. I'm so happy that things turned out okay for you. I know it was rough going there for a while."

"So, is something up, Nick? Is there a reason for a call rather than just a text?"

"Are you dating anyone?"

Dean was silent for a long moment. "Um...are you asking me out?"

"Huh? Oh no. I'm going out with Gabe now."

"Gabe Griffin? That cute Southern boy?"

"That would be him. We haven't been going out all that long, and he's really sweet."

"He has a cute brother, too." Dean paused. "Jared. He was always nice to me."

"Yeah, Jared's a decent guy."

"So why do you want to know whether I'm seeing someone?"

"I have a favor to ask of you. Would you be willing to go on a blind date? The boy's name is Tyler, and he's quite good-looking—curly blond hair, blue eyes. I think you'd like him."

There was a pause. "I've never been on a blind date before. So does he go to our—I mean your—school? I don't recall anyone by that name."

"No, he goes to Itona High, the same school as Ericka Spooner's girlfriend."

"Ericka Spooner is gay? No shit! I would never have guessed that one."

"Yeah, who would have guessed, hey? So you see, here's the thing. Tyler's boyfriend, Tony, died a little over a year ago and since then, Tyler's been severely depressed, dropped out of pretty much everything. So I thought that the attentions of a hot boy like yourself might bring him around."

"I dunno. You know that I'm not what one would consider outgoing, right? I don't even go on dates with people I know."

"I know this is a lot to ask," said Nick. "But there's a little more to this than just a simple date."

"Like what?"

"As I said, since his boyfriend's death, he's totally withdrawn into himself and is keeping everyone at arm's length. His friends are worried sick about him, so we're trying to get him back out there again."

"I can relate. I've been there myself."

Nick nodded. "So we're hoping meeting new people might pull him out of his shell."

"And you want me to go out on a date with this kid who's super depressed?" He sucked in a sharp breath. "I dunno if this is something I'd feel comfortable doing."

Nick stewed on Dean's words for a moment. "It would help Tyler a lot. And who knows? Maybe you'll end up liking each other."

"Nick, I truly appreciate what you did for me and my family. But this sounds a little too intense for me. I don't even date people who *aren't* depressed."

Nick's heart sank, but then a sudden idea came to him. "How about if I come with you?"

"You'd come with me on a date?" Dean asked. "Don't you think that'd be a bit weird, being a third-wheel and all?"

Nick chuckled. "No, I mean like a double-date. I'd come along with Gabe."

Dean breathed what sounded to be like a sigh of relief. "Okay, I guess. As long as you and Gabe come along as backup, I'll do it."

"I'll try to set it up with Tana and will get back to you with the time and location."

After they disconnected, Nick thought about calling Tana right away, but figured he'd better ask Gabe first. Nick hadn't planned on a double-date. He'd hoped that Dean would be willing to go out with Tyler on his own, but Nick couldn't blame him for being hesitant. It was a lot to ask of someone.

The idea of going out with a depressed kid who had an angry ghost hanging around him didn't appeal much to Nick either, although Dean didn't know about the angry boyfriend. If Dean had known, Nick guessed that there would have been no way he'd have agreed to go. Nick probably should have told Dean the truth, but if they were lucky, Tony wouldn't make an appearance, so it would not be an issue. If they were lucky.

Given that Dean went through a tough time himself when he was at their school, Nick figured that he and Tyler would have something in common. But now, upon reflection, Nick wondered just how good of a plan this truly was —trying to fix up a couple of downhearted dudes? Maybe this isn't the best idea in the world.

GABE AND NICK sat cross-legged in the middle of Nick's bedroom floor, facing each other. Nick's phone was plugged into his speakers through which was coming instrumental guitar music that Nick was streaming. He wanted the music to be loud enough so that his parents couldn't hear what they said, yet not so loud that his mother would come to complain. Confident that his parents were downstairs and occupied, Nick shuffled closer to Gabe. Gabe flashed a warm half-grin, the same one that always caused Nick's heart to skip a couple of beats.

Gabe leaned in and pressed his lips lightly to Nick's. Nick closed his eyes, sinking deeper into the warm kiss. Gabe broke the kiss, and they pressed their foreheads together. Gabe pulled away first.

"Is your door locked?" Gabe whispered.

Nick shook his head. "They'd get suspicious if I locked the door. I never lock it."

"Then we shouldn't."

"I know." Nick sighed. "I just missed the hell out of you."

"Me too," said Gabe. He intertwined his fingers with Nick's. "So you wanted to ask me something?" Gabe wagged his eyebrows at Nick, a mischievous look on his face.

Nick gave Gabe a playful swat on the arm. "Nothing like that, you dirty-minded boy." Nick had texted Gabe earlier and asked if Gabe could stop by because he had something important to ask him. "Remember the ghost I told you about at the prom?"

Gabe nodded. "The one who was hanging around that curly-haired kid? Tyler, wasn't it?"

"Yeah. I talked to Tana, and she told me all about the situation with the kid. Apparently, the ghost was Tyler's boyfriend." Nick then filled him in on everything Tana had told him. "So then I had the idea to call Dean Ridelli."

"Ridelli? I didn't know you were still in contact with him after he left our school."

"I'm not. His step-father gave me Dean's cell number."

Gabe stared intently at him. "Okay, I'll bite. So what does Ridelli have to do with prom ghost?"

"Seeing that Tyler was so depressed, I thought maybe going out on a date would help."

"Help who? The ghost or Tyler?"

"Both, actually. I have this strange feeling that Tony's presence around him is keeping Tyler from moving forward."

Gabe creased his brow and then narrowed his eyes. "Didn't Katrina tell you not to get involved with ghosts? I thought it was dangerous because of that shadow demon."

"She did, and it is. Hence, I thought I'd try an alternate plan, one that doesn't entail any involvement with me and the ghost."

"Did Dean agree to it?"

Nick nodded. "But only if we go with him. He said that he'd be more comfortable if it were a double-date type of situation. I can't really blame him. Tony is kinda scary."

Gabe looked at him in a you've-got-to-be-kidding-me kind of way. "No."

Nick reared back. "What do you mean, no? It's just lunch at a cafe with Dean and Tyler. It's no big deal."

The flush of anger on Gabe's face startled Nick. He certainly hadn't expected this reaction.

"How can you say it's not a big deal?" Gabe said through gritted teeth. Nick tensed the moment he said it. "You yourself agreed that getting directly involved with a ghost could endanger your life. Sure, I can see fixing up Dean with Tyler. That makes sense. Kind of. But what doesn't make sense is that you have us tagging along. You've already interacted with this ghost once. He knows you can see him. I'm sure he's not going to simply ignore you if he shows up. Didn't he warn you once to stay the hell away from him and his boyfriend?"

Nick took a deep breath and crossed his arms over his

chest. "I met him briefly, only for a moment, and he probably won't even remember me. I don't plan on acknowledging him at all. I figured that we'd be there as support for Dean." Nick swallowed. "Besides, Dean won't do it unless you and I are along."

Gabe threw his arms in the air, stood up and then plopped himself down at the edge of Nick's bed. Nick rose and turned around his desk chair so that it faced the bed and sat down. Gabe refused to meet his eyes.

Nick cleared his throat dramatically. He dropped his gaze. "Will you do it?"

"It's dangerous."

"I know."

"You promised."

"I know, but..."

"What about what Katrina said? What about the demon thing?"

Nick thought it best not to tell Gabe about the ghost he had crossed over at Katrina's store yesterday. "I won't interact with the ghost at all. As I said, I'll pretend that I don't see him."

Gabe slowly shook his head. "I don't like this, Nick, not at all. You swore to me you wouldn't put yourself in any danger. For God's sake, this thing is killing psychics—like you! Or have you forgotten about that?"

Nick took a deep, unsteady breath. "No, I haven't forgotten. I hadn't planned on us coming along. I had hoped Dean would go alone and perhaps distract Tyler, thinking his boyfriend's ghost might then cross over. I only want to help them."

Gabe met his gaze. "I know you do." His voice was considerably lower now, almost a whisper. "But I'm scared. Scared for you, scared for me."

"I am too. And I've been masterful at not acknowledging ghosts when I see them. You have no idea how difficult this is—but I plan on continuing to ignore them. That's why I'm trying something different this time. Now, it may or may not work, but I need to give it at least a shot. I can't just let this poor kid unravel because of a ghost."

"How do you know he's unraveling because of a ghost? Maybe he's in mourning. I can't imagine how long it would take me to get over it if anything ever happened to you."

"I think it's more complicated than that. When I saw them at the prom, the ghost was so overly possessive and seemed intent on keeping everyone away from Tyler. That might be why Tyler's so withdrawn and has cut all ties with his friends. I have a hunch that this ghost is preventing anyone from getting close to the boy."

Gabe raised his eyebrows. "When you say you have a hunch, do you mean like one of your psychic feelings?"

"I dunno, I guess so. It's hard to say where the feelings come from. Both Katrina and my uncle told me to listen to my gut. Well, my gut is telling me that Tony is suffocating Tyler."

Gabe stared at him for a long moment. "And you won't communicate at all with the ghost if we go?"

Nick shook his head. "Nope. I'll pretend I can't see him."

"If he threatens you, confronts you or otherwise speaks to you, we leave immediately. I don't care who in the hell he is or who he's tormenting. We will not risk your life for an aggressive teenage ghost."

Nick blinked. "So you'll do it? You'll go?"

Gabe's eyes held him. "As long as you promise."

"I promise."

"I mean it, Nick."

"So do I. I swear. Really."

Before he could say anything else, Gabe stood up. He filled his lungs and eyed Nick with frustration before giving in. "Okay, I'll do it. But I don't like it, though I suppose it's good that I'll be there to keep an eye on you. I know you. You're not to be trusted."

"If we go. The date's not yet a sure thing. We still have to convince Tyler to go."

Gabe raised his eyebrows. "We?"

"Tana and I. Remember she goes to the same school as he does?"

Gabe nodded. "I was wondering how you were going to contact Tyler. I forgot about Tana."

"She called me a couple of days ago to tell me about Tyler. I had asked her about him after the prom."

"That was nice of her." Gabe's voice had a chilly edge to it.

"She's trying to help."

"Was the date with Dean and Tyler her idea?"

Nick shook his head. "It was mine. After she told me all about Tyler and what had happened to him, I knew I had to do something."

"Even if it puts your own life in jeopardy?"

"Gabe..."

Gabe placed his hand in a never-mind gesture. "Let me know once you set the date and time." With that, Gabe opened Nick's bedroom door and left without turning to say goodbye.

CHAPTER FIVE

"Mind if I sit with you?" Nick whispered to Ericka. It was study hall period, and Ericka sat alone at a large table. A couple of the other kids gave Nick a strange look, perhaps wondering why in the hell a nobody like him was pestering Ericka Spooner. Nick and Ericka definitely did not run in the same circles.

She smiled and indicated to a chair with her head. Nick pulled it out and sat down right next to Ericka. Now everyone, including the study hall monitor, looked at him strangely.

"I got your text," Nick asked. "You said you wanted to talk to me?" Nick wondered why she just hadn't told him what she wanted in her text. Instead, she asked him if she could talk to him at school. He hoped she didn't want to go on another double-date. Not that he didn't have a good time at the prom, but again, he didn't want to attract any undue attention to himself and risk that the school would figure out that he and Gabe were an item.

She closed her geometry book and looked over both her shoulders. She then locked gazes with Nick. "Tana told me that she set up a date with Tyler and some other kid. I'm curious as to what's going on. I thought you didn't know Tyler before the prom."

"I didn't," Nick said. "I mean, I don't. Not really. I just felt bad for him, from what Tana told me about him. I know someone who's in the same boat as Tyler, so I figured it might help if they got together."

"Who? Is it someone from his school?"

"No, he was originally from ours, but he transferred to a different one."

"Do I know him? What's his name?

"Dean."

Her eyes widened. "You don't mean Dean Ridelli, do you? The weird goth kid?"

Nick winced. "That's the one. He lost someone recently, so he's going through something similar."

"Ridelli lost a boyfriend?"

"No, both his parents."

"Ouch. But still, Nick, I dunno about this. Ridelli is kind of a freak. Do you think this date thing is a good idea?"

Her words stung. "It's true that Dean was going through some tough times while he was here. But now that he's at the new school, he's much better. You'd hardly recognize him. He's even on the swim team."

She studied his face for a moment. "I still don't understand why you're so concerned about Tyler, someone you don't even know."

"It's not just Tyler. It's also Dean. This might be good for the both of them."

"I didn't know you hung out with Dean Ridelli. I don't recall him hanging with anyone. While he was here, he was kind of a loner, wasn't he?"

"I knew him a little bit," Nick said. "We talked a few times, and he e-mails me occasionally."

She pushed her book to the side, folded her hands, and rested them on the table. She leaned forward, ever so slightly. "I know you think you're doing a good thing here. And maybe you are. But I'm not too fond of Tana getting involved with this. These kinds of things tend to backfire, and I don't want her to have to clean this up."

"I didn't mean to involve her," Nick said. "I didn't know how else to contact Tyler."

"Look," she said, a serious look on her face. "I still don't see why this is so important to you. I don't get it. Why try to fix up a kid who you don't know with another who goes to a different school? Why is Tyler any concern of yours?"

Nick shrugged. "All I want to do was help. When Dean was here at our school, I failed him. We all did. He was grieving, but instead of helping him, people bullied him—bullied him to the point where he felt like he couldn't face another day at our school. I feel like I should've done something to help him at the time. I figured fixing him up with Tyler might do them both good. Tana tells me that Tyler's having a pretty rough time of it."

"You are right about Ridelli. Someone should have shut that shit right down." She gave him a weak grin. "I don't mean to grill you or anything. I guess I'm a bit overprotective of Tana. I don't want the kids at her school figuring out she's gay. She wouldn't handle that well at all."

"I thought nobody knew that Tyler's gay?" Nick whispered.

She shrugged her shoulders. "People talk. People figure things out." She narrowed her eyes. "You're a nice kid, Nick, and I get what you're trying to do. I can feel for Tyler.

Hell, I don't know what I'd do if I ever lost Tana. I just don't want her to get into any kind of trouble, you know?"

He nodded. "I get it. I promise I won't involve her anymore with this."

She laughed. "Yeah, good luck with that! She now thinks she's little Miss Matchmaker and is dying to see how this all turns out, Tyler's date with Ridelli. I'm sure she'll be calling you to find out the details—even though it's against my better judgment."

"I'll let her know if they like each other but won't ask her for anything else."

She raised her eyebrows. "But how will you....ah, that's right. You're in contact with Ridelli."

"I'm also going along on the date."

A look of curiosity crossed her face. "Come again?"

He chuckled. "It's going to be a double-date—me, Gabe, Tyler, and Dean."

She winked at him. "Another one? So you have a thing for double-dating now, do you?"

He shook his head. "Not really. It was the only way Dean would agree to go. He's a bit shy."

She creased her brow. "Does Tyler know that you and Gabe are going as well?"

Nick thought for a moment. "Now that you mention it, I don't think I told Tana that we were coming. I just asked her if she could somehow convince Tyler to go for coffee with a friend." He rubbed his chin. "I hope this all doesn't freak Tyler out."

"I don't see why it would," Ericka said. The hall monitor walked by their table, and Ericka picked up her book, pretending to study. Once he was past, she put the book back down. "You simply introduce yourself as Dean's friends. I'm not sure if Tyler even considers it a date. Tana just told him she has a friend she wanted him to meet. Not sure how she did it, but she somehow got him to agree. Although it's not surprising—she has a strange way of being able to convince anyone to do anything." She pursed her lips. "You know that Tana had to come out to Tyler because of this, right?"

Nick grimaced. Now he understood why she was so pissed about him involving Tana. Nick couldn't see himself coming out to anyone—not quite yet. And yet, somehow, he'd just come out to Katrina. But telling someone at his school would be an entirely different matter. "I'm truly sorry, Ericka. I didn't intend for that to happen."

"How did you think she was going to convince Tyler to go out on a date with a boy?"

"But didn't she know him from the GSA? Wouldn't he already have known she was gay?"

"She was there only once, quite awhile ago. She didn't go back, afraid of outing herself to the school, I guess. After reflection, she decided she wasn't ready to take that step and would instead keep her head down until graduation. She was pretty sure no one remembered her. Tyler certainly didn't, from what she said—he barely seemed to notice anyone but his boyfriend back when he was at the GSA." All at once, her eyes turned mindful. "She did tell me something weird about Tyler, though."

Nick leaned in closer. "Weird?"

She nodded. "It's kind of the reason I don't want her around him. When she asked him if he'd be willing to meet another gay kid for coffee, he mentioned his boyfriend a couple of times. The dead boyfriend, Tony. But what's strange was that he talked about him as though he were still alive."

Nick was chilled, yet fascinated. "Are you sure he mentioned him by name?"

"Definitely. Tana said it creeped her out. He stressed that it was only for coffee and not a date because he didn't want to piss off his boyfriend, Tony. Now, is that strange or what?"

Could Tyler see ghosts? Or did he somehow know that his dead boyfriend was still hanging around? "That *is* creepy. And you're sure he's talking about Tony Fisher?"

"Positive." Nick waited, but she didn't elaborate.

"What makes you so sure?" Nick asked.

"Tana asked him how long they've been dating, and he said a little over two years. It has to be the same Tony who died. Now you understand why I don't want her around him? Yeah, I know he's grieving and all that, but pretending your dead boyfriend is still alive? That's fucked up."

"Wow, I had no idea. I swear I won't ask Tana to do anything else like this." He drew an X over his chest with his finger. "Promise."

The sweet smell of chocolate drifted through the room, meaning someone in the room was discretely eating a candy bar. At that moment, Nick would have killed for a Snickers.

"I'd appreciate that," she said, pulling Nick out of his chocolate reverie. She smiled. "But let me know how it turns out with Tyler and Ridelli. I guess I'm kinda curious too—although if Ridelli had any sense, he'd run screaming from Tyler."

Or from Tyler's boyfriend, Nick thought.

"MOM? DAD?" Nick called out. He noticed his mom's car was gone, but he still wanted to make sure neither of them was home. He listened for another minute and then threw his backpack on the chair next to the dining room table. He pulled out his Tarot deck. It was time to do a reading about this, to see if he should involve himself any further.

He shuffled seven times, as was his custom, and asked what he needed to know about the Tyler and Tony situation. He then laid out three cards on the table.

He turned over the first card.

The Emperor. This was a card of control and power. But who was in control? Nick didn't think it was Tyler. On the contrary, Tyler was quiet and withdrawn, at least according to Tana. No, Nick guessed that the Emperor represented Tony. Was Tony controlling Tyler to such an extent that Tyler still acted as though Tony were alive?

He turned over the next card.

The Hanged Man. This card depicted a man hanging upside down from a tree by his ankle and represented stagnation or being stuck. Nothing was moving; nothing was happening. Nick knew right away that this card depicted Tyler, especially in light of what Ericka had told him. Tyler was stuck in an imaginary relationship with his deceased boyfriend, desperately hanging on to what they once had. That would certainly explain why the ghost hadn't crossed over. Nick remembered his uncle telling him that sometimes people refuse to let their loved ones go, which can prevent a spirit from crossing over. Was this the case here? Was Tyler holding on so tightly that he was stopping Tony from crossing over?

Nick turned over the third card.

Two of Cups. This card depicted a man and a woman, each holding a large cup and touching hands. This was a card of romance, and it represented bonding or attraction, sometimes harmony. His uncle had called it *the date card.*

Nick stared at the image. Why are the cards telling him everything he already knows? He knows that Tony and Tyler were a couple, and they obviously loved each other. So why show him this?

Nick held up the card and squinted, and as he did, a new idea popped into his mind. The people in the card almost looked as though they were making a deal with each other, like a contract or a business deal. Maybe that's why their hands are touching. Perhaps they're shaking on an agreement, and the cups they're holding represent the celebration of the deal. Did Tony and Tyler make some sort of agreement with each other that extended after death?

Nick shuddered as he recalled his encounter with the angry ghost at the prom. Tony obviously didn't want anyone near Tyler. But for what reason? Nick would have thought that he'd want Tyler to move on so Tony could cross over. Nick decided that he'd somehow broach the subject when they met for coffee.

He studied the three cards. They didn't tell him all that much more than he already knew. Although the appearance of the Two of Cups was curious and Nick couldn't get the idea of an agreement out of his head. What in the hell kind of deal had the two of them made?

Nick scooped up the cards and shuffled them back into the deck. For the moment, the cards weren't talking; or if they were, he didn't understand what they were telling him. Perhaps he'll be able to discover more once he met Tyler in person. He just hoped Tony stayed away.

Just as he shoved the deck into his backpack, the doorbell rang. Must be Gabe. Nick glanced at his phone, surprised at how late it was. It was time to go on their double date.

CHAPTER SIX

THE TRAY of luscious-looking fruit pies in the window of the cafe caused Nick's stomach to rumble. The little black and white cardboard signs informed him that there were blueberry, raspberry, strawberry-rhubarb, and triple-berry blast. Pie. He couldn't think of the last time he'd eaten a piece of sugary fat-laden fruit pie. His mom was not a fan of any type of pie, so if by chance there were any sweeties in the house, they tended to be cake or ice cream—and even then, only on special occasions. However, dessert was the exception rather than the rule, so Nick typically had to get his goodie fix away from home.

He breathed a sigh of relief when he saw that Gabe was already at the restaurant. He was seated at a table outside the cafe, which Nick thought was a good idea. Less chance of someone overhearing them. As he reached the table, he noticed a large piece of pie with dark red filling sitting in front of Gabe. The crust looked extra flakey, with a light sprinkling of sugar on top that glistened in the sunlight.

"What are you eating?" Nick asked, pointing to the dessert.

Gabe smiled when Nick sat down. "Triple-berry! If you want any, you'll have to go inside and get your own 'cause I ain't sharing any of mine." Nick breathed a sigh of relief. Gabe no longer seemed too pissed at him. Or if he was, he was hiding it well.

"Maybe I'll wait for Tyler and Dean."

Gabe snatched his phone off of the table and glanced at the screen. "Plenty of time. They're not gonna be here for another twenty minutes." He put a forkful of pie into his mouth and then groaned with pleasure.

Nick's mouth watered. "In that case, maybe I will snatch a piece. When I mentioned to Dean that we were meeting at Miss Ruby's Pie Shop, he said he'd sworn off desserts. Doesn't want to gain any weight, I guess. So if I want pie, it's now or never."

The inside of the cafe was surprisingly empty, with only four or five tables occupied. A sweet smell of peaches and sugar hung in the air. Nick inhaled deeply, which made his stomach rumble all the more. He ordered a slice of raspberry pie and a cup of American coffee. He nearly dropped the coffee while trying to open the front door, using one hand to hold his pie and hot cup.

"So what kind did you get?" asked Gabe, as Nick sat down.

"Raspberry."

"Yum. That was my second choice." Nick noticed that Gabe's pie was gone.

"So no sign of them yet?"

Gabe shook his head. A large bright red splotch splayed across Gabe's cheek.

Nick pointed to his own cheek. "Um...you got a little something there."

"Oh," Gabe said, blushing. He rubbed his face with his napkin. "Did I get it?"

Nick nodded. "All gone."

Gabe looked at the napkin, chuckled when he saw the big red streak on it, and then placed it on top of his empty pie plate. "You sure that Tyler said he was going to come?"

"That's what Tana told me. He didn't seem too crazy about the idea, though. She said that he stressed that this was not a date."

"Truth be told, I wouldn't cry any tears if neither of them showed up. I'm not too keen on this wild plan of yours."

Nick closed his eyes for a moment. "I know you aren't. I appreciate your willingness to do this."

Gabe gave him a lazy smile, the kind of smile that made Nick's heart thump louder in his chest. "This isn't just about me, you know. I'm worried about you. Yeah, I probably overreacted a bit yesterday, but there's a reason for it." He took a big gulp of his coffee. "I had a dream that the shadow demon killed you, and it scared the shit out of me." Moisture glistened in Gabe's eyes.

Nick wanted to grab Gabe's hands, but resisted. They were, after all, out in public—and Gallowspine Mountains was a small town. He leaned in forward, closer to Gabe. "Why didn't you tell me?" Nick said in a low voice. "Why keep something like that from me? You're the one who's always saying no more secrets."

Gabe avoided Nick's gaze and nonchalantly wiped his eyes with his sleeve. "It just freaked me out so much, and I didn't even want to think about it, much less talk about it. It seemed so damned real. This whole thing is scaring me, with those mediums getting killed and all." Gabe turned and locked eyes with Nick. "Have you heard anything from Nate?"

Nick's jaw tightened. "Not for a while, nothing since he told me about the meeting in France."

Gabe raised his eyebrows. "When is that again?"

"Pretty soon, I think. I'll fire off an email to Nate in the next couple of days to see if there's any news."

Nick heard the shuffling of boots behind him. He turned.

"Hey, Nick!" It was Dean. Though his black hair was still spiked, he wasn't as gothed-out as he'd been before he moved. He was wearing a faded pair of jeans, a yellow t-shirt, and ankle-high chunky black boots. It was the first time Nick had seen him wearing anything but black.

"How's it going with you? Long time no see." Nick gestured to the empty chair next to him. "Have a seat. Unless you want to get a drink or some pie."

Before he could answer, Gabe said, "I don't know if you know me. My name's Gabe Griffin."

Dean nodded. "I've seen you around. I know your brother Jared—he was one of the few people at school who was always kind to me."

"Yeah," said Gabe. "Jared's a good kid. So what'll you have? My treat."

"You don't have to—"

"No problem at all."

"Harumph!" Nick said. "You didn't offer to treat me."

Gabe narrowed his eyes and turned his gaze to Nick. "Just being around me is treat enough for you."

Dean laughed. Just then, Nick's gaze caught sight of Tyler coming down the sidewalk. His eyes were glued to the ground, and he looked jittery, nervous. The ringlets of his curly blond hair hung just below his ears, shimmering and bouncing as he walked. He wore dark blue New Balance sneakers that looked nearly new, a crisp pair of skinny black jeans, and a gray T-shirt with red lettering—though Nick couldn't make out what it said, since the black hoodie he had on covered part of it. His skin was pale and smooth, and his full lips had a pinkish hue. Nick could definitely understand what Tony saw in him. He was cute. Tiger Beat cute.

"I think Tyler is here," Nick said.

Gabe and Dean both turned to look down the sidewalk. Tyler must have sensed that they all were watching him as he looked up abruptly. Nick gave him a wave. Tyler stopped for a moment, looking uncertain, then eyes glued to their table, approached slowly.

"Hey," he said. He studied all three of them. "So, which one of you is Dean?"

"I'm Dean. Can I get you something from inside?"

"Not right now," Tyler said. He looked at Nick and Gabe. "I don't think I know either of you. Which one of you knows Tana?"

"We both do, actually," said Nick. "We went to the prom with her and her girlfriend Ericka."

Tyler raised his eyebrows. "You went to the prom? As a couple?"

"We went to the prom, but not with each other," said Nick. "Well, we did, but we didn't. I pretended I was with Ericka, and Gabe's date was Tana. It was a weird situation."

"But fun," said Gabe.

"I saw you at the prom," Nick said.

Tyler visibly stiffened. "Going was against my better judgment. I just wasn't feeling it. I'm not much of a prom guy." He turned his regard to Dean. "Were you there too?"

Dean shook his head. "I go to a different school, but even so, I wasn't gonna play the prom game."

Tyler studied Dean's face for a moment. "Cool hair, by the way."

"You, too," Dean said. "I've always wished I had curly hair. You're lucky." He leaned back in his chair. "So, what do you do for fun?

He shifted in his chair. "These days, not too much. Mostly hang out at home."

"Have you been here before? To this cafe?"

Tyler shook his head. "It just opened not too long ago. I heard they have good pie."

Nick turned his head and met Gabe's stare. They both smiled. All at once, Nick's breath left his body, and his stomach lurched so much so that Nick clumsily leaned forward. He felt the quick sweep of vertigo. He grabbed onto the side of the table as cold seeped into his spine. His skin felt like it was being poked with thousands of tiny cactus needles simultaneously.

Ghost.

Nick jerked his head to face Tyler. Standing directly behind him, arms crossed and wearing an extremely pissed-off expression, was Tony Fisher. His face was so red that it was almost glowing.

His eyes were like blue ice, and his gaze tore into Nick. "What in the fuck is this?"

Nick kicked Gabe under the table and mouthed the word "Ghost."

"Don't you dare ignore me, shithead!" the ghost screamed in a piercing voice that skewered Nick's eardrums. The words flew out of the ghost's mouth, fast and ruthless, like a sniper's fire. "I remember you, and I know

damned well you can see me. Are you the one who orchestrated this whole thing?" He made a grand sweeping gesture
with his hand. "Huh? I know Tyler would never do this on
his own. What is this supposed to be, some kind of a date?"

Nick's entire body stiffened, and it was only with the
greatest effort that he resisted looking at the ghost. He
stared intently into Gabe's eyes, praying that if they ignored
the ghost, he would go away. This was exactly what he'd
been afraid of, and seeing Tony again made him question
how he ever thought this was a good idea. Time froze for an
interminable moment.

"Nick, is something wrong?" asked Dean. "You don't
look so good all of a sudden."

"I don't think the pie agreed with me," Nick said, his
voice shaking as he spoke. He thought about leaving and
taking Gabe with him but didn't want to leave Dean alone
with the angry spirit.

With a whoosh that caught Nick off-guard, Tony
popped in directly in front of Nick, his face only inches
away from Nick's. Nick gasped and reared back with such
force that he nearly tipped over his chair.

"Nick!" cried out Gabe. "What is it?"

But the expression on Gabe's face told Nick that he
knew exactly what was wrong.

Slowly, Nick raised his eyes to meet Tony's. The
menacing coldness of the ghost's stare chilled Nick so much
that his body shivered involuntarily. He tried to hold on to
his gut as the contents within them roiled.

"Ah, that's better," said the ghost in a voice that was low
and seductive. "Now, you will answer me. Why is Tyler
here?"

"We're just having a friendly cup of coffee, nothing

more," Nick stammered. Nick heard Gabe mutter "Fuck" under his breath, and from the corner of his eye, Nick could see that Dean and Tyler were staring at him wide-eyed.

The ghost pursed his lips in a fierce snarl. "And there's four of you, just like a double-date. Isn't that sweet?"

"Why don't you just go away and leave us alone," Nick said recklessly. "You don't belong here."

"*What did you say to me?*" said Tony. His words cut sharply, like an axe in a tree.

"I said—"

Before Nick had a chance to finish, the ghost bent over, and with an arm that seemed to grow in length, brushed all the plates, cups, napkins, and silverware off the table in one quick swoop. There was a loud crash as the items hit the sidewalk.

"Oh no, not again," Tyler said, a look of fear on his face. He stood up so fast that his chair tipped over. There was a loud crunch as he stepped on a piece of broken glass. "I'm sorry, this is all my fault."

He turned and ran.

"Wait," Nick cried out, but as he stood up to run after him, the ghost pushed him back down. Nick's breath left his body.

"This is the final warning," the ghost said in a fierce whisper, a pale finger pointing at Nick. "*Stay the fuck away from Tyler.* If you don't, bad things will happen. Trust me when I say this."

He then disappeared. Nick could tell immediately that the spirit was gone. His stomach returned to normal, and the tingling in his skin ceased. Dean and Gabe were both standing, their hands firmly affixed to the table.

"Wh...what was that?" Dean said. His voice trembled as he spoke. "What just happened?"

"That would have been a ghost," Nick said. Dean knew from personal experience that Nick had the ability to see spirits that haven't yet crossed over.

Dean's eyes widened. "There was a ghost? Here?"

Nick nodded, but remained silent, trying desperately to calm down.

"I'm guessing that was Tyler's boyfriend?" asked Gabe.

"You guessed correctly," said Nick.

"Tyler has a boyfriend?"

"Used to," said Nick.

"He died," said Gabe.

"And is very pissed-off," said Nick.

"Wait," said Dean. His voice was harsh. "You knew about this? You deliberately set me up on a date with him, knowing that his menacing ghost boyfriend was around?"

Nick looked down. "I'm sorry. I thought it might help Tyler."

"Help him?" Dean exclaimed, pushing away from the table. "What about me? About us? We could have been hurt!"

"I didn't think he could do that," said Nick, eyeing the scattered debris from their table on the sidewalk. "They usually can't. Move things, I mean. Well, some of them can, but only the super angry ones. I guess Tony Fisher is one of those really angry ones."

Dean's expression hardened even further. "I'm done with this. Don't try to fix me up with anyone again. Why in the hell I agreed to this, I have no idea." He turned and started walking away.

"Dean, wait!" Nick said, but Dean held up his hand in a don't-talk-to-me gesture and kept walking.

A moment later, the door to the cafe flew open, and a man, who was apparently the owner or manager of the cafe, ran out. "What in the hell is going on here? You punks are going to pay for these broken dishes."

Gabe released a loud sigh. "So that went well."

"Don't," Nick said. "Just don't say anything."

"My lips are sealed."

NICK CONVINCED his mother to write him a note to excuse him for a couple of hours from school during lunch break and study hall. He explained that he wasn't going to miss any actual classes and would be back well before his physics class after study hall. His mom was amazingly cooperative, especially considering the amount of school he'd missed last semester. She had looked at him and asked, "So why do you need to miss classes?" and all Nick had to say was that it was ghost-related. His mother had nodded and written him the note. Upon handing it to him, all she said was, "Just don't make this a habit—and be careful."

He crossed his fingers as he entered the Itona High School grounds and tried to calm his shaking hands. He didn't know why he was so nervous. It wasn't the first time he'd wandered around a strange high school, and he would not be in any danger. Or at least he hoped not. Who knows what might happen if Tony shows up. The ghost had demonstrated yesterday that he could move physical objects and, if he chose, could even cause people harm. Nick hadn't been hurt by a ghost yet, though he'd come close. Thus far, experience has shown that he had more to fear from the living than the dead.

It was lunchtime, and according to Tana, Tyler usually sat off by himself outside. He'd quit the school lunch program and started bringing his own food, always eating it under the same tree when the weather allowed. The temperature was warm for May, so Nick prayed that Tyler would stick to his habit. He'd prefer not to have to go into the school building and try to hunt him down. Schools don't take too kindly these days to strangers wandering the hallways.

Nick turned around the corner and spotted Tyler leaning against the tree, just as Tana said he would be. He held a sandwich in his hand and was staring off into the distance. Nick breathed a sigh of relief at not seeing any sign of Tyler's dead boyfriend. Nick briefly glanced over his shoulder to ensure that the ghost wasn't behind him and slowly approached Tyler. Tyler was gazing off in the opposite direction and didn't notice Nick as he drew near.

Nick crept a little closer to the kid. A bright red apple, shiny and untouched, sat on a brown paper bag right next to Tyler. Nick's stomach rumbled, reminding him he hadn't eaten anything since this morning.

"Tyler?"

Tyler snapped his head around and met Nick's gaze. He looked confused for a moment, as though he were trying to figure out who Nick was and why he was talking to him. Then, a look of recognition dropped over his expression. His body tensed up, and he stuffed the sandwich in the paper bag, knocking over the apple in the process.

"You! You were at the cafe yesterday."

Nick nodded. "I need to talk to you."

Tyler groaned in annoyance, picked up the apple and placed it into the bag. He looked like he was getting ready to leave. "If this is about yesterday, I have nothing to tell you."

Nick held out his right hand, palm forward. "Wait, don't go yet. Just give me a minute. Please."

Tyler studied Nick's face for a moment and then

frowned. "Okay, one minute." He put down the lunch bag. "So, what do you want?"

Nick swallowed hard to coax the saliva back into his dry mouth. "I want to talk about what happened yesterday at the cafe."

"I told you, I have nothing to say. It was windy, and I freaked out. I'm sorry I left without saying goodbye. I've been kind of stressed out lately."

"Tyler, I know what really happened."

Tyler's head swung around as though he were looking for someone. His frown deepened. "I don't know what you're talking about. I said I apologize that I was so rude."

"Tyler, I know it was Tony who caused the dishes to fly off the table. I know that—"

Tyler interrupted Nick with sudden fury. "You don't know what you're talking about! Just what kind of game are you playing? Tony's dead. There's no way he could have been there. What kind of asshole are you?"

He made to get up, but Nick rested a hand on his shoulder and gently coaxed him down, surprising himself by his audacity. He plopped down on the ground next to him. Tyler refused to meet his eyes.

"I know he was there," Nick said. "I saw him. I also know that he used to be your boyfriend."

Tyler stared at Nick, wide-eyed. He opened his mouth to reply, but Nick pressed forward.

"I saw him at the prom. He was there with you, dressed in a blue mechanic's suit. Then I saw him again at the cafe. He's very possessive of you. That's why the big scene yesterday. I think he might have been jealous that you were out on a date."

Tyler studied Nick's face for a long moment and then

let go of a prolonged, slow breath. "You can see him? Like in person?"

Nick nodded. "Yes."

"But how? How come you see him, but I can't?"

"I dunno exactly how it works," Nick tried to explain. "It's an ability that some of the guys in my family have. My uncle could see ghosts, and so could my grandpa."

"Ghosts," Tyler repeated with a sudden nervous insistence. "You can see other ones too, besides Tony?"

"Sometimes. But only the ones who haven't crossed over."

"You mean like go to Heaven?"

"Something like that."

Tyler scooted closer to Nick. "How is he? Tony, I mean. Does he look okay?"

"He looks fine, except that he gets pissed off when anyone gets close to you. You knew he was there yesterday, didn't you? It's happened before."

Tyler sighed. "I always felt that Tony was around me, but I was never sure. I just assumed that I thought so because I missed him so damn much—that it was my imagination or wishful thinking. However, I catch random glimpses of movement out of the corner of my eye sometimes. Once, I was studying at the library with Ryan, this guy from my Spanish class. I had no idea that he was gay, and I think he started hitting on me. All of a sudden, my Spanish textbook flew off the table and smacked Ryan right in the face. I'd never seen anything like it. Ryan was so freaked out that he took off without saying anything. He kept his distance from me after that. I honestly think he believes I threw the book at him."

Nick nodded, suppressing a chuckle. "That makes sense. Tony does come across as quite the jealous type."

Tyler smiled faintly. "He always was. For some reason, Tony had this fear that I was gonna run off with someone else. I couldn't fathom why he thought that or where it came from. Tony was the most handsome guy you could ever want. He was also sweet and generous." Tyler wiped his wet eyes with his sleeve. "I don't think he knew how much I loved him."

"Did he ever hurt you?"

His brow darkened. "What? No, never. He never once hurt me or anyone else that I'm aware of. He was a little insecure, that's all. Tony quit school to stay home and take care of his dad, who had to have a couple of surgeries. Because he didn't finish school, he was always afraid that people considered him stupid. He planned on returning once his dad got better."

That's good to know. "So now you have the opportunity to help Tony."

He cocked his head curiously. "Help Tony? But how?"

"We need to help him cross over?"

Tyler's face blanched. "You mean, talk him into leaving?"

Nick nodded. "When people pass away, they're supposed to leave, to move on to the next phase of their journey. They're not supposed to remain here, where nobody can see them."

Tyler slowly shook his head. "No."

Nick reared back and looked at Tyler, startled. "What do you mean, no? Maybe you don't understand. What I was—"

"I understand perfectly." Tyler blinked, and the blood drained from his face. "I'm sure if Tony wanted to go, he would have. Instead, he chooses to stay here. With me. Now that I know for sure Tony is here, I'm certainly not going to help you make him leave."

"But Tyler —"

"I love him. I love having him around me. You know, I can always tell when he's around. It's like I'm in this dark place and I'm afraid. Then suddenly, that fear disappears. I feel safe, and I know deep inside that it's because of Tony. Tony's always made me feel safe. No, I'm gonna neither force him nor encourage him to leave."

Nick didn't expect this reaction at all. "It's wrong, Tyler. He can't stay here."

Tyler shook his head quickly, impatiently. "Tony is the only thing that keeps me going. I'd hate to think of where I'd be without him."

"Tyler, you are without him. He died. He's no longer here. You need to let him go so he can cross over."

Tyler darted to his feet. "Just leave me alone. Hell, I don't even know your name."

Nick stood up. He considered offering his hand to shake, but decided against it. Tyler didn't seem like the hand-shaking type. "Nick Michelson."

"Well, Nick Michelson, you can forget it," Tyler said, sounding even more hostile now. "I am not making Tony leave so you can mind your own business. What I do is no concern of yours."

With that, Tyler took off running. Nick debated going after him when, all at once, he shivered. He felt as though he had just stepped into a walk-in freezer. He then heard someone behind him laughing.

He spun around, but there was nobody there. The laughter grew louder.

"Tony? I know you're here."

The laughing stopped, and almost immediately Nick's

body temperature returned to normal. The ghost was gone. He'd obviously heard what he and Tyler had discussed. Shit! Now that he knew Tyler was aware of his presence and wanted him to stay, there was no way Nick could convince him to cross over. Maybe it's time for Nick to walk away from both of them and this situation. Let them both do whatever in the hell they want. He was done with them.

CHAPTER SEVEN

"I was beginning to suspect that you'd blown me off," said Katrina, as Nick came through the front door. Her head was in her hands, propped up by her elbows, which rested on the counter. "Or did you forget that you have a reading scheduled?"

"Sorry. No, I didn't forget about the reading. I got hung up at school."

"I hope not literally."

"Huh?"

"Never mind. Are you ready to get to work?"

"Yup." He put down his backpack behind the counter and pulled out his Tarot deck. Nick found the soft tick-tock of the old-fashioned wall clock soothing. "This time, I will use my own cards."

"Good, Nicholas. It's always best to use your personal deck whenever possible."

Nick shot a glance toward the dark-purple curtain in the back of the room. Nick could have sworn that it was black the last time he was here. "Is she already here, the client?"

Katrina crossed her arms. "And why do you think it's a she? Is it only women who seek guidance?"

Nick shrugged. "I just assumed—"

"Never assume. Most assumptions are stereotypes and have no place in a healing environment."

"So it's a dude then?"

"Yes, your client is a gentleman, and no, he's not here yet. He called requesting a male reader. Luckily, I now have one on staff."

"Can I talk to you before he gets here?"

"Certainly. What's on your mind?"

Nick swallowed. "I haven't been entirely honest with you."

She raised her eyebrows. "Oh? How so?"

Nick broke from her gaze. "About the ghost thing. I've had contact with a spirit recently. A couple of times, in fact."

"Nicholas....." She took a deep breath and sighed. She placed an uncomfortable gaze on him. "Even though you know how dangerous it is? That doing so could end up getting you killed?"

"I know. It just kind of happened."

"Of course. That's how it goes. Encounters with spirits always just kind of happen. We never go out of our way to find them. They find us." She clasped her hands together and rested them under her chin. "Where did you encounter this ghost. At school?"

"At the prom. He was hanging around this kid that goes to Itona High School. Apparently, it's the ghost of his boyfriend who drowned a year ago."

She sat in silence for a long moment. "So sad. So the ghost wants you to pass on a message to his boyfriend. What's the boyfriend's name?"

"Tyler, and the dead kid is Tony. But no, not exactly."

She raised her eyebrows. "No? What does he want then?"

"He wants me to leave them alone."

She eyed him over her glasses. "If the specter doesn't want your help, then why are you involved?"

"This Tyler kid is supposedly taking the death of his boyfriend pretty hard. He keeps to himself now and has dropped out of all the things he used to enjoy. I dunno. I had a bad feeling about him and wanted to help."

She cast him a dubious stare. "Wait...let me get this right. *Nobody* asked you to help? Neither the ghost nor the bereaved?"

"Um...I guess not. When Tana told me Tyler's story, I felt like I had to do something, especially after encountering his aggressive boyfriend. Let me tell you, he's a genuine piece of work, that one. A major asshole." Nick looked away and sighed. "You're right, though. It's none of my business. I should never have gotten involved."

"Do not go putting words in my mouth, young medium. I said nothing of the sort. I'm just trying to get a handle on how you got involved with this. Usually, it's a ghost who comes to a medium for help. It's rare for a medium to try and help a ghost who doesn't want help."

"When you put it like that, it does sound stupid, doesn't it? But it's not the ghost I'm trying to help. It's Tyler. It just felt wrong somehow that this spirit was hovering over the kid and not letting anyone get close to him." Nick told her about the disastrous date at the cafe with Dean, as well as his encounter with Tyler and the ghost at Tyler's school.

She deadpanned him. "You've certainly been a busy boy, Nicholas."

Nick stilled. "And that's what I needed to talk to you

about. What you said is true. Neither of them asked me to help. I butted into something that was none of my business. Tyler said he's content with the way things are and doesn't want Tony to cross over. Tony wants to hover around Tyler and not cross over. So I'm done. I've decided to let them be and leave them the hell alone. This way, they both get their wish." He told himself that he would no longer butt into Tony and Tyler's life, even though the entire situation broke his heart.

"Don't you think it's too late for that?"

Nick creased his brow. "Why do you say that? I haven't done anything yet except piss people off."

The door opened, and the bell above the door rang. A brightly dressed middle-aged woman with two white shopping bags came in. She gave Nick and Katrina the quick once-over.

"Good Morning," the lady said and immediately headed over to the herb section.

"Good Morning," Katrina responded. "My name is Katrina. Please let me know if you have any questions."

"Is that my client?" Nick whispered.

Katrina shook her head. "I already told you that your client is male."

"Oh. Right."

"Now, back to your ghost situation," she said, lowering her voice. "I believe you've done more here than you think you have. You've pointed out to both of them that what they have isn't right—and that Tony doesn't belong here anymore."

Nick considered this briefly. "But both of them pretty much told me to piss off. Why not just let them go on as they have been?"

Katrina rubbed her chin. "Because these sorts of things

never end well. The dead cannot have a romantic relationship with the living. It never ever works, and it often ends
up fatal for the living partner."

"Fatal? Like dying kind of fatal?"

She clasped her hands and rested them on the counter.
She took in a deep breath. "Is there any other kind? Yes,
dying fatal. The partner left behind is often so heartbroken
by their inability to be with their deceased loved one that
they try to follow them in death." She paused and studied
Nick's face. "I'm sure you don't want this for your young
friend Tyler.

Nick thought about her words. Tana said Tyler had
been depressed ever since Tony died. But now that he
knows Tony's still here, would he try to join him?

So you don't think I should let them go on as they have
been?" Nick asked.

"Watch the word 'should,' Nicholas. Don't try to give
your power to me."

"Oh yeah, right." He scratched his forehead. "So it may
be in the best interest of both Tony and Tyler for me to
continue helping? Or at least try to?"

She laughed. "That's better. But as always, such a decision is entirely up to you."

"Hey! You're supposed to be my mentor."

"And I'm mentoring you. I'm leading you to make your
own decisions."

He folded his arms, annoyed. "I was hoping you'd tell
me what to do."

"I know you were."

He sighed. "I don't know what to do. If neither of them
wants help, then I'm not sure what I can do. I don't want to
force myself on them."

"I can understand your hesitation. And we must not

forget that there is the issue of the shadow demon. It's still out there and remains a very real and dangerous threat. I'd like to tell you to stay far away from this ghost, but this does sound like a serious situation for the living young man involved. Have you asked the cards?"

Nick shook his head. "Kinda. I did a reading on it a couple of days ago, but it didn't tell me much of anything. So I wanted to talk to you. Before I came here, I had pretty much decided to do nothing, to let Tyler and Tony be. Truth be told, I was almost positive that you'd tell me to stay away from them because of the danger."

"That was—and is—my first instinct." She swallowed and sighed. "I don't like the idea of you making yourself vulnerable to this demon, but we don't want to take a chance that Tyler may hurt himself, either. This is a tough call."

"So, what do you think? Will I regret it if I try and help them? Will I regret it if I don't?"

She chuckled. "Why don't you do a reading on it? Try asking what the outcome might be if you help and what it might be if you don't. Often, the cards can provide a different perspective—a different way of looking at the situation."

"I think I will. Speaking of cards, what time is my reading?"

She glanced down at her book. "In about five minutes. Nervous?"

He ran a hand through his hair. "A little. Last time it was easy. The ghost told me what to say. This time, I'm going in cold."

Katrina snorted. "I hardly think you're going in cold. Your intuition is strong, and you're a whiz at the cards. You'll do fine."

Before Nick could respond, the door opened, and a muscled young man with short-cropped blond hair wearing military fatigues walked into the store. He glanced around nervously before noticing Nick and Katrina at the counter.

"May I help you?" Katrina asked.

"My name's Dillon. I have an appointment."

"Ah yes, for a reading. Nicholas, why don't you take your client to the reading room."

The man eyed Nick doubtfully. "You're doing the reading? You're such a young dude."

"I assure you that Nick is a very gifted reader," Katrina said.

"Sure, why not?" Dillon said. He gestured with his hand. "Lead the way."

Nick could feel his heart rattling in his chest. He'd never read for a guy before, especially not one who was a soldier. Still, it wasn't his first close encounter with a soldier —just the first who was actually alive.

He sucked in a deep breath and concentrated on stopping his hands from shaking. Okay, so he'd lied to Katrina. He was, in fact, nervous.

Once in the back room, Nick took his seat and then gestured for the man to sit down. Instead of sitting across from him at the opposite end of the table, the man took a chair that was against the wall and dragged it, so it was right next to Nick's, and then plopped down. Nick considered telling the man that it was customary for the client to sit across from the reader, but stopped himself. He was the customer, so he could sit wherever he wanted. He actually liked that the client sat right next to him. It's seemed much more personal.

"So, what brings you to see me today?" Nick could hear the tremble in his own voice.

"My girlfriend," Dillon said. He folded his hands on the table. "I want to know if she's going to come back to me."

Nick recalled both Katrina's and his uncle's lessons on rephrasing a question. He hoped this would work. He didn't want the guy to think that he asked a shitty question.

"The Tarot doesn't do well with yes and no questions, as we often have the ability to change the outcome of a situation," Nick explained gently. "How about if we instead ask, 'What do I need to know about my relationship with my girlfriend?' This might even give you more information."

Dillon shrugged. "Sure, you're the boss. Her name is Rebecca. Becky."

Nick nodded and shuffled the cards. He said out loud, "What does Dillon need to know about his relationship with Becky?" Damn, this was a lot easier last time when he had a ghost telling him what to say.

Without thinking, Nick laid out four cards face down on the table. All at once, he realized that he'd forgotten to assign each card a position. He briefly considered starting over again, but didn't want to look like an amateur in front of this man.

He turned over the first card. *The Empress.*

The first thing that popped into Nick's head was 'Mother.' "This card represents mother energy, and The Empress is the ultimate earth mother. She might even be pregnant." *Now, where did that come from?*

Dillon stared at Nick, expressionless. Nick turned over the next card. A man lay face down with a bunch of swords stuck in his back. *10 of Swords.*

Nick looked at the Empress card and then at the 10 of Swords. In his mind, he saw a doctor's office with several young women sitting in a waiting area. A nurse came out and called out a name. A young woman stood up and accompanied the nurse into a room. "You will need to change into a hospital gown before your procedure." The young girl nodded. Tears ran down her face.

Nick shook the vision from his head and met Dillon's gaze. "I don't know how to ask you this, but did Becky have an abortion?"

Dillon's eyes grew wide. "How in the hell could you know that?"

Nick pointed at the cards. "The 10 of Swords next to the pregnant Empress. The 10 of Swords suggests that there was perhaps a painful ending of some sort, and being next to the Empress, tells me that it might have been a pregnancy. The appearance of swords can also sometimes point to surgery."

Tears filled Dillon's eyes. "We talked and talked about it. I wanted to keep it. She didn't. I wanted to be with her. She told me she wasn't sure how she felt about me. We finally decided that having the operation would be the best thing. I had no say in the matter." He wiped his eyes.

Nick nodded and said nothing. He turned over the third card. 3 *of Swords.*

Nick stared at the card and bit his bottom lip. Three swords pierced a bright red heart. Surrounding the pierced heart were several black and menacing-looking storm clouds. Heavy rain filled in the card's background.

Nick took a deep breath, trying to figure out the best way to tell the dude that his girl is probably not coming back. "The 3 of Swords is a card of heartbreak, often points to a painful breakup." Nick swallowed. "Or the end of a relationship."

Dillon met Nick's gaze. "After the operation, she said that she no longer wanted to be with me, said that she could never feel the same way about me as she did before. She broke it off—just like that. I never saw it coming."

"I'm sorry," Nick said. "That must have been very painful and difficult for you."

"It was." Dillon sucked in a sharp breath. "But is there a chance she'll come back to me? She said that she had to think things over for a while and get herself together. Once she does that, will we get back together?"

Nick turned over the last card. 8 *of Cups*. A figure was walking away from eight cups abandoned on the ground, and by the looks of it, he wasn't coming back.

Dillon stared and then pointed at the card. "What does this mean?"

Nick closed his eyes for a moment and then reopened them. "This is a card of moving on—cutting off old emotional ties and bringing in new ones."

Dillon's body shook. "So what you're saying is that she's not coming back? She's left me for good?"

"It looks like that might be the case. But let's pull one more card for advice." Nick remembered Katrina saying that she always pulls an advice card at the end. She also said never leave a client in a worse place than they were before they came. Reading must empower an individual, not disempower them.

Dillon nodded, but stayed silent.

Nick shuffled and turned over a card. *Two of Cups*.

"This card signifies a partnership—of two people coming together, often in a new relationship. There is a mutual physical attraction." Nick pointed at the card. "Does this make any sense to you? Is there someone that you are attracted to and who might be attracted to you?"

Dillon blushed. "I dunno. Well, there is this one woman. She might have flirted with me a time or two, but I wasn't sure." He pursed his lips. "Plus, I was hung up on Becky, so I didn't give her too much thought."

Nick tapped the Eight of Cups card on the table. "Maybe it's time for you to move on too."

Dillon stared at the cards and then at Nick. He sighed. "You're right. It's been over with Becky for a while now. I keep waiting and waiting, hoping something will change." He sighed. "It might be time to give someone else a chance."

Nick nodded. "This last card is a good omen. Both of the people in the card look shy, like they're afraid to say what's on their mind. Maybe if you took the first step?"

Dillon met Nick's stare. "And ask her out?"

Nick scooped up the cards and placed them on top of the deck. "Why not? I have an inkling that she'll say yes."

Dillon nodded. "Thank you so much for this." He stood up. "You know, I never believed in this stuff until now. I know that Becky used to get readings done, so I figured I'd try it out." He held out his hand. "You are the real deal, little dude. I'll be back next time I'm in town; you can be sure of it."

Nick stood up and shook Dillon's hand. Dillon followed him out of the room and into the main store entrance, where Katrina watched both of them out of the corner of her eye.

"You were right," said Dillon. "He knows what he's doing. He told me things that nobody else could have known. I'm glad I came."

Katrina smiled. "I'm so glad you had a pleasant experience. Nicholas certainly is one of a kind."

After he left, she turned to face Nick. "So I take it the reading went well?"

Nick nodded. "It was great. Once I saw all the cards together, I could read his story. I knew exactly why he came and how it probably would turn out."

"And no ghosts?"

"Not a one." Nick tapped his forehead. "This all came from my own little brain."

Katrina chuckled. "I prefer to think of it as coming from spirit, but whatever works for you. But today, you've helped me in confirming my suspicions."

Nick raised his eyebrows. "What suspicions?"

"That you are much more than a simple medium, though I've long suspected as much. You also have a powerful psychic ability, with an especially strong penchant for the cards. I suspect your uncle guessed this when he gave you his deck."

"But didn't we already know that from the visions I get?"

"Yes and no. Your visions tend to come on unexpectedly, and from what you've told me, you typically have little or no control over them. Today, however, you've demonstrated that you can focus your ability and call it forth when needed. That's an impressive skill, my friend. You're not only a gifted medium but also a talented psychic as well."

Nick looked at the floor. "Thanks, I guess. It kinda comes out of nowhere."

"Yes, it does seem so at times. So this is your second professional reading for a client. Are you feeling more confident now?"

"If it's always this easy, then yeah, I'm feeling confident."

She slowly shook her head. "No, it's not always going to be easy. Even if the information comes readily, sometimes it will be difficult to pass those messages on to your client. There's a lot more to reading than parroting back information."

"How so?"

"You also have to learn how to empathize with your clients and to deliver their messages in the gentlest manner possible, and that is a skill in and of itself. And then there are those clients who do not want to hear the truth, who will refuse to believe anything you say. These people are the most challenging."

"Got it. But I think I did pretty well today."

"I agree. Do you remember what I told you about clients leaving your office?"

Nick nodded. "They should always be in a better place when they leave than they were when they arrived. I actually thought about that during the reading, which led me to pull an advice card. It made all the difference."

She smiled. "Such an excellent student you are, Nicholas. Knowing this might help you when a problematic situation arises. That will be the real test."

NICK ROLLED his scooter into the garage, maneuvering around four white boxes of books, a large orange snow-blower, his dad's long red sea kayak, two yellow wheelie bins, the electric lime green electric lawnmower, a wide silver-colored snow scoop along with numerous shovels, an aluminum bin filled with bird food and other various debris such as tools, rakes, gasoline cans and camping equipment. His father had mentioned to Nick a couple of times that he wanted him to clean the garage, but so far, he hadn't gotten around to it. This weekend, for sure. It was getting more and more challenging to find an empty spot to park his scooter.

He placed his half-helmet on the shelf next to his full-face helmet, picked up a soft rag and wiped his helmet's shield in an attempt to remove the bug carcasses that he'd gathered on the way home. He had nearly finished when his skin prickled, and his stomach slammed him so hard that he dropped the cloth he was holding and took a wobbly step back. The room seemed to have cooled thirty degrees instantly.

There was a ghost here.

But why was it in his garage?

Nick jerked his head and looked behind him. Nothing. He turned back, and standing right next to him, only inches away from his face, was Tony Fisher, Tyler Tarrant's deceased boyfriend. Nick screamed at the ghost's unexpected appearance and lurched back, crashing into the shelf against the wall. A box of Christmas decorations hit the floor with a loud crash.

"WTF, dude!" said Nick. "You scared the shit out of me!" He held up his arms in front of his face and backed away. "I don't know why you're here, dude, but I haven't seen Tyler or been anywhere near him. You both can do whatever in the hell you want. I promise I won't go near him again. So leave me alone."

The spirit glanced over his shoulder, not giving any indication that he had heard what Nick said. He stared nervously down the driveway.

"Did you hear me?" asked Nick, peeking through his fingers.

Tony snapped his head toward Nick. "Do you see anyone else?"

"Huh?" It was then Nick noticed how stiff and tense the ghost appeared, almost as though he were afraid.

"Is there anyone else here besides us?"

Nick could see fear all over the ghost's face, which

seemed out of character for him. "No, there's only you and me. No other humans or spirits."

"You're absolutely sure?" the ghost stammered.

Okay, so now he was being Cryptic Man. "Positive. Now, will you tell me what's wrong?" Nick was still unsure whether he could trust Tony.

"There's someone after me. I don't know who it is. All I could see were these gray shadows. They grabbed onto me, and I could feel them trying to drag me somewhere. I don't know where or why. I got away from it and came here."

Nick's entire body stiffened with the news, and his mouth grew dry. "Shadows? Was it another ghost?"

"Maybe. I don't know. I couldn't see a face. I was at a bookstore with Tyler when all of a sudden, there it was. Before I could even react, it was all around me, suffocating me, pulling at me. I could tell it was trying to drag me away. I put up one hell of a fight and somehow managed to escape the thing. It was so strong. It made me feel so cold."

Nick felt his apprehension rising. "Did it say anything? Or tell you what it wanted?"

Tony shook his head. "It didn't speak at all. Never said a word. It just encircled me and felt like it was trying to crush me." Tony's eyes grew wide. "Was it the devil? Was he trying to take me to hell?"

That was a good question. His uncle had told him about the light that spirits go into when they cross over. But what about the evil ones? Did they go into the light as well, or did some other entity claim them? He'd have to ask Katrina.

"I don't honestly know," said Nick. "But I don't think so. I've seen nothing resembling what you described. I think it might be something else."

"Like what?" the ghost choked out. "Do you know what it is?"

"Not exactly. But people are investigating it."

"So you know what I'm talking about! You've seen it!"

Nick rapidly shook his head. "Not personally, no. But others like me have seen it." Nick swallowed. "And unfortunately, things didn't turn out so well for them."

He peered at Nick with steely eyes. "What do you mean?"

"All I know is that it's killed several people. It seems to be targeting people like me, those of us who can see ghosts."

"But why did it attack me?" Tony asked. "I never was able to see ghosts. Hell, I don't even know if I can now—see other ghosts, I mean. What did it want?"

"I wish I knew. There are some people in Europe who are working on trying to figure out what this thing is and how to vanquish it. So far, everyone's been calling it *The Shadow Demon*."

The ghost's eyes grew wide. *"There are such things as demons?"*

Nick shrugged. "Nobody knows if it's really a demon or what it even is. It's just what they've been calling it, for lack of a better name."

The ghost shot Nick a sharp look. "So what do I do? How do I keep it away from me?"

Nick brushed his fingers through his hair. "Keep your eyes open and maybe try not to stay in one place too long. I'll e-mail my French contact and see if he has any ideas. This is the first I've heard of it attacking a ghost." Nick swallowed, feeling guilty for telling the lie, but he wanted to calm the ghost down. He thought it best not to tell him that the entity has tried to snatch spirits as they're about to cross over. Tony relaxed, but just barely.

Nick decided to steer the conversation away from The Shadow Demon. "Can I ask you a personal question?"

Tony furrowed his brow. "Sure. What is it?"

"How did you pass away exactly? I'm sure my friend will want to know. It might give him an idea about why you were attacked."

Tony held his gaze. "I drowned."

Nick nodded. "Is there anything else you remember? Were you alone?"

Tony nodded. "Yes, I was all alone. I'd decided to go for a swim and..." He stopped, and his expression darkened. Then his eyes lit up with excitement. "Wait. That's not right. I wasn't alone. There was someone with me!"

"Who was it?"

Tony held Nick's gaze for several moments. "I can't remember. Damn it! But I know there was someone else there. I recall going down there with someone. Weird. This is the first time I've remembered that."

"So you didn't go to the park by yourself? This person came with you?"

Tony nodded. "I think so. I remember us being there together... I'm pretty sure. But maybe I'm wrong. My memories are still all so muddled." He scratched his head. "Wait, who called in my death?"

"A stranger who was walking his dog," Nick said. "At least that's what all the articles I've read stated."

"Oh," said Tony. He gazed absently over Nick's shoulder. "Then I probably was alone. Funny though, I could have sworn that there was someone else there besides me that day—someone that I knew. Dammit! I wish I could remember."

"Do you think it's possible that you might have been murdered?"

Tony looked stricken. "Murdered?"

Nick nodded. "That might be why whoever you were

with didn't call the authorities. Maybe he or she wanted you dead."

He creased his brow and narrowed his eyes. "I don't recall. All I can remember is sinking underneath the water and not being able to breathe." He leveled a hard stare at Nick. "But why would someone want to kill me?"

"That's what we'll have to figure out. That might be why you're still here. It could be the reason why you haven't crossed over."

Tony nodded. "And you'll ask your friend about the shadow thing?"

"I'll e-mail him this evening. Until we find out more, be careful. If you see anything out of the ordinary, get out of there as quickly as possible."

"Agreed," said the ghost, and with that, he vanished.

Nick sighed loudly. He pressed a large blue button on the wall, and the garage door noisily descended. He pulled the keys out of his pocket and fumbled, trying to unlock the door with trembling hands.

This was not good. So the Shadow Demon was no longer only in Europe but was now here — and was close. He wondered if the monster already knew about Nick, since he'd been in contact with Tony. It was too much of a coincidence that this thing was now at his front door.

For the first time since hearing about this entity, Nick was truly frightened, right down to his core. It had never seemed quite real before. It was always something that was far away and not really an immediate threat.

But now all that seemed to have changed.

CHAPTER EIGHT

It was after 11:00 p.m., and Nick still hadn't sent an e-mail to Nate. After Nate warned him that getting involved with ghosts was too dangerous—and that he might attract the Shadow Demon—Nick had promised to avoid all contact with spirits. So what had he gone out and done? Not only had he made contact with a spirit, but he'd also inadvertently attracted the demon—though Nick wasn't sure if it even knew about him. It might be a coincidence that the same sort of shadow thing attacked Tony.

That's all it was. A coincidence.

His uncle's voice rang in his mind. *"There's no such thing as a coincidence, Nick."*

Nick remembered his Uncle Mitch saying this to him. Didn't Katrina say this to him once as well? But maybe they were wrong.

Yeah, right.

Nick pressed the latch on his laptop, and the lid popped up. With his touchpad, he clicked the icon for his e-mail program and began typing. In the message, he confessed everything—how he'd been helping Tyler and Tony, and how that led to Tony getting attacked by something that sounded eerily similar to the entity that had been killing Nate's friends: other mediums like him.

He clicked Send, and a few minutes later, his phone rang.

"Nick?" a strange voice said.

"This is Nick. Who's this?"

"It's Nate, calling from France. I got your message."

This was the first time Nick had ever spoken to the man in person. Up until now, they'd only corresponded via e-mail. His voice sounded a lot younger than Nick would've imagined.

"What time is it there?" Nick asked.

"About 6:20," Nate said. Now Nick could hear his accent. "Can you tell me anything more? Was there anything that stood out about the demon that your friend Tony might have noticed?"

"He said it seemed to come out of nowhere and then completely surrounded him. He said he felt as though it were trying to drag him somewhere."

"Did it communicate with him at all?"

"No. He told me it didn't say a single word to him."

"Are there any other details you can recall? Anything you can tell me may help."

"Tony didn't see much, only shadows, I think. It engulfed him, and then it tried to pull him away. He somehow escaped and came to see me. He was pretty shaken up by it."

Nick heard Nate sigh into the phone. "That is disturb-ing. This is the first I've heard of the thing showing up in the United States and attacking a spirit that wasn't in the process of crossing over. So I take it you've been in contact with the ghost, this Tony then?"

Nick swallowed. Here it comes. "Yeah, a couple of times. I've been trying to convince him to cross over but so far, no luck."

"Even though you're aware of the danger involved? Even after we've all warned you not to?"

Nick hesitated. "I'm sorry, I wasn't thinking. I only wanted to help Tony and Tyler."

"Yes, Katrina told me you were stubborn. Who's Tyler?"

"Tony's boyfriend. But he's still alive and is having a tough time in letting Tony go."

"That does tend to happen. What disturbs me is that the Shadow Demon assaulted a ghost you're helping. This leads me to suspect that the demon may be aware of you and could be using your ghost friend to get to you. I cannot chalk this up as mere coincidence."

"Why me?" Nick choked.

"Why any of us?" said Nate. "He has attacked and killed mediums indiscriminately." There was a long pause. "But *you* may hold a special interest to him. So I figured it was only a matter of time."

"Because I'm a medium, too?"

"Yes, and because of your abilities. Over the past several years, many psychics have foretold the arrival of an especially gifted medium—and based on what your friend Katrina has told me about you and your abilities, my instincts say you might be that medium. If this demon is indeed trying to prevent spirits from crossing over, then it may see you as a special threat."

"You think it knows about me?"

"It's possible. I don't believe it was a fluke that it confronted a ghost you were helping. It may be trying to get to you."

"So, what do I do?"

"Has anyone taught you how to protect yourself from malevolent entities?"

"You mean like protection rituals?"

"Exactly."

"Yes, Katrina has taught me a bunch of them. I try to protect myself every time I leave the house."

"Good. This may be the reason the entity hasn't confronted you directly. Perhaps he's been unable to find you because of your protections. But Nick, you must be even more dedicated from now on. If it finds you, it will wait for when you are most vulnerable. Thus, you must reinforce your protections throughout the day as often as possible. I can't overstate the importance of the practice, Nick. *This entity must not find you.*"

Nick swallowed. "I will. I promise." Why did Nick feel as though there was something Nate wasn't telling him?

"You must be extra vigilant as well. Always be aware of your surroundings, and if anything looks or feels off-kilter, get out of there. If you see the entity, do not confront it or try to communicate with it. Don't go anywhere near it."

"Got it." Nick sucked in a breath. "Do you have any idea yet what this thing might be?"

"We have our suspicions. You are familiar with the Other Side, correct?"

"Of course. It's where the ghosts go when they cross into the light."

"Correct. But there are other realms as well. Darker realms. We encounter entities from these realms from time to time, but mostly, they are confused and lost spirits, those who had gone through a difficult incarnation while they were alive. We suspect that this entity may be from one of these such realms, and it has taken it upon himself to—how shall I say this—collect souls."

"Why would it collect souls?" Nick asked. "What would it get out of it?"

"What most malevolent entities want—power. Apparently, this demon is strong enough to kill people and snatch spirits as they're trying to cross into the light. We suspect he may be a ruler of one of these realms, and the more spirits he can control, the more powerful he becomes. I've read allusions to this in old books, but they've lacked any specifics that could be helpful. I'm guessing snatching the souls of psychics may render him even more powerful because of their ability to communicate with the Other Side."

"Do you think he's killing us in order to entrap us in some sort of dark realm?"

"We suspect this may be the case, yes. Additionally, we help spirits cross over into the light. That's not what he wants—so the more mediums he murders, the fewer wayward spirits cross over, and the more there are for him to snatch."

"Scary."

"Scary indeed," Nate replied. "So you understand why it's important that you do not attract the attention of this spirit?"

"I'll be careful." Nick paused for a moment, then asked, 'How does someone go about killing it—or vanquishing it, or whatever it is you do to get rid of demons?'

"We have a few ideas. I'll let you know more after the meeting here this month. Are you sure there's no way you can attend?"

"I wish I could. But there's school and a lack of money."

"Understood. I'll be in contact with you. And Nick?"

"Yes?"

"Please try to limit your contact with any spirits until

you hear from me. It's too dangerous now that this thing is so close to you."

"What about Tony?"

"That ghost you're helping?"

"Yeah. He seemed pretty scared."

"I understand that it's in your nature to try to help—we're all this way—but you're going to have to leave this one alone. He's apparently caught the attention of the demon, possibly with the end goal of trying to get to you. Going anywhere near this spirit could provide the access to you that the demon is hoping for. This is important, Nick. You *must* stay away from him."

"I understand," Nick said.

"I'm sure your parents would agree with me. What do they think of your involvement with Tony and his partner?"

"Um..."

"You have told your parents about this, haven't you?"

"Not really, no. They don't like to talk about things like this."

"Regardless of whether or not they want to talk about it, you must have this conversation. It's important for them to know that they could be in danger as well."

"But why would the demon go after them? Had it hurt non-psychics in the past?"

"Not that I'm aware of. But it may use any means necessary to get to you. If you are with your parents and the thing attacks, they might get caught in the crossfire. Perhaps you could teach them how to invoke the protection wards?"

Nick laughed. "Nate, there's no way in a million years they'd do anything like that. They barely talk to me about this stuff. I'm certain they'd never go around chanting protection spells."

"Don't be too quick to judge them, Nick. It might

surprise you what people will do should the need arise, especially when the safety of their family is at stake."

They said their goodbyes, and Nick tossed his phone on top of his desk. Tell his parents about the demon? That would go over like a turd in a punchbowl. He's not sure if they'd actually believe him, though they know that Nick helps ghosts, so he supposed they'd believe in a demon as well.

The more he thought about it, the more he suspected that perhaps Nate was right. If there was any possibility that they could be in danger because of him, they had a right to know. And what about Gabe? Gabe knew about the demon, and until now, Nick never even considered the possibility that the Shadow Demon could be a threat to him. He'd have to teach Gabe the protection rituals as well. Hopefully, Nick's parents and Gabe will be willing to learn the protection spells. Nick just hoped none of them would ever have to actually use the things.

THE DOOR SWUNG OPEN, and a musty smell attacked Nick's nostrils. It had been a week since he'd been to the cabin—his uncle's house—which now belonged to him. Nick was allowed to stay there overnight on weekends, which he hadn't done so far. He'd come to clean and hang out there a few times but always returned home at the end of the day. It was way too creepy to sleep there by himself—to be all alone in a secluded cabin in the woods. At home, he found it reassuring that there were other people in the house. You'd think someone who talks to ghosts wouldn't be such a wuss.

Nick opened up all the windows to let in some fresh air.

His mother had made him promise that he'd do a weekly cleaning of the cabin and not allow it to deteriorate to a state similar to his bedroom. He promised her he would and thus far had managed to keep that promise. Even though he was now the official owner of the cabin (which, in actuality, was more like a small house), he still considered it to be his uncle's, and he knew how much his Uncle Mitch hated disorder. So Nick kept the cabin clean and clutter-free, just like his uncle had done. The last time his mother had accompanied him to the place to give it a once-over, she'd nearly fallen over from shock. Orderliness was not in Nick's nature.

Nick swept the floors and then took a Swiffer to them. While the floor was drying, he curled up in the bed and began reading one of his uncle's Tarot books that was on the bookshelf next to the large oak dresser. He'd only gotten through a few pages when goosebumps crawled up his arms. His gut lurched.

Nick put the book down and looked around. Nothing. But Nick was sure there was a ghost nearby. His senses never failed him. His breath was harsh in his throat.

"Uncle Mitch?"

"Nope, sorry." The sudden voice next to him caused Nick to jump. Tony stood next to the nightstand, arms crossed over his chest.

"Dammit, Tony. Don't do that. Ever."

"You're pretty jumpy for a dude who can talk to the dead."

"I wasn't expecting anyone to pop into my room unannounced," Nick said, meeting the ghost's gaze. "How'd you find me here, anyway?"

Tony narrowed his eyes. "I can find you anywhere, Nick. You give off majorly strong vibes."

Oh great, thought Nick. *So much for hiding from the demon.*

Nick nodded. "You okay?"

"If you mean have I had any run-ins with the thing that attacked me, the answer is no."

Nick breathed a sigh of relief. "That's good. Hopefully, it's gone for the moment." Nick sat on the edge of the bed. "So, what do you want?"

"I want you to help me."

"Help you how?"

"I'm ready to cross over," said Tony. He crossed his arms over his chest. "I've given a lot of thought to what you said, and you're right. It is time for me to let Tyler live his life."

Nick recalled his promise to Nate that he would not involve himself any further with this spirit. Nick was about to tell him that he couldn't help him, but changed his mind at the last moment. What's one more crossing? And hopefully, with Tony gone, the shadow demon would have a more difficult time finding Nick. Given that Nick had started this whole thing—had gotten involved without asking—he owed it to both Tyler and Tony to see it through.

"So, when do you want to leave? How about now?"

Tony's eyes shifted away for a moment. "Not quite yet. First, I want to say a proper goodbye to Tyler. I have a feeling that's what will make the light appear so I can move on. But I can't do that on my own. I need you to help me."

"So what, you want me to translate for you?"

Tony nodded. "Yeah, I guess that's a good way of putting it. Since I can't verbally communicate with Tyler, I need you to tell him what I want to say."

Nick briefly considered this. "What is it you want me to tell him?"

"I'll let you know when we're all together. I need to

think about it a little bit more." He put on a lazy smirk. "Will you do it, then?"

Nick hesitated. "I guess—but we need to do it as soon as possible. It also has to be somewhere private. How about Tyler's house?"

Tony shook his head. "His parents are home pretty much all the time." He looked around the room and smiled. "How about here? It's secluded, and there's nobody around to hear us."

He let out a long, slow breath. "If Tyler's willing to come here, then I guess I'm okay with it. How about tomorrow afternoon? Can you be here then?"

Tony's smile widened, and his eyes gleamed. "I can be here whenever you want me to. You'll have to call Tyler and let him know where and when. Do you have his number?"

"My friend Tana got it from him the time we met at the cafe. But getting Tyler to agree to this might be a problem. My conversations with him never seem to go all that well."

He locked eyes with Nick, and Nick felt a shiver run up his spine. "Once you tell him that I want to speak with him through you, I'm sure he'll agree. But don't let him know that I'm going to be crossing over."

"Why not?"

Tony shook his head. "If you do, he'll never agree to come. This is going to be difficult enough for him as it is. Tell him instead that I only want an opportunity to talk to him in person."

His stomach soured. Nick felt in his gut that something was wrong with this plan, but he had no idea what it was. Maybe it was his instincts telling him that it might be difficult getting Tyler to agree to a meeting. Or perhaps the light wouldn't appear for Tony. Or worse yet, perhaps his instincts were warning him that the Shadow Demon might join them as well. This meant that he'd need to double-up on the protection rituals that Katrina had shown him. Nick didn't want to risk the demon finding him here at his uncle's place. He only hoped that Tony wouldn't draw the monster to them.

"I'll call him tonight. But if he says he won't come, I'm not gonna to push him. Deal?"

The ghost stared at him impassively. "Agreed. But you promise you'll try? Really try?"

Nick nodded. "I'll do my best. I want you to cross over just as much as you do. It'll be the best for everyone involved."

"Especially Tyler," said the ghost. But Nick didn't think Tony sounded all that convincing, but before Nick could add anything, he was gone.

CHAPTER NINE

"Let's sit here," Gabe said, pointing to a log that was in front of them. After Nick had talked to Tyler, he'd called Gabe and invited him to the cabin. He needed someone to talk to about this stuff.

A cardinal sat in the lowest branch of the red oak tree next to the cabin and was chirping continuously with a steady *wheat-wheat-wheat* sound. A large bumblebee buzzed near them but didn't come too close, much to Nick's relief. Though he wasn't allergic, he avoided getting too close to bees. When he was a kid, he stepped on a dandelion on which, as it so happened, a bumblebee was perched. Nick could still feel the pain as the bee stuck its stinger into the tender bottom of his foot.

"So let me get this right," Gabe said after they both had sat down. "Tyler sounded excited to come to the cabin tomorrow? The same surly kid who screams at you every time he sees you?"

Nick nodded. "I know, right? I told him that Tony wanted to talk to him, to pass on some messages to him, and the only way he could do that was through me."

"How'd you get his number, by the way?"

"Tana gave it to me when she set up our coffee date."

"Ah yes, the infamous coffee date." Gabe chuckled. "I'm surprised he didn't hang up on you the moment he heard your voice."

"I was afraid of the same thing, and truth be told, I'm pretty sure he was screening my calls. I left a voicemail, and he called back a few minutes later. The last time I talked to him, he made it clear that he didn't want me anywhere around him."

"So he was okay with Tyler crossing over?"

Nick broke Gabe's gaze. "Um...well...I didn't exactly tell him that Tyler was crossing over."

Gabe studied his face as though trying to gauge his intentions. "What do you mean you didn't tell him?"

"Tony thought that Tyler would refuse to come if he knew the real reason for the meeting—and I agree with him. Tyler's holding on pretty tightly to Tony. I don't think he'd be too keen on the ghost crossing over and losing him for good."

"In other words, you're lying to him," Gabe said.

"It's not exactly lying. I told Tyler that Tony wants to talk to him, and that's the truth. I just didn't tell him about Tony's intentions. That'll be up to Tony to do that."

"I could see this not going well."

Nick creased his brow. "How so?"

"It's going to be quite the shock for the poor kid once he figures out what's really going on. He'll think you orchestrated the entire thing."

"But crossing over the ghost is the best thing for the both of them," protested Nick. "Even Katrina told me that it's not healthy for Tyler to continue holding onto Tony the way he is. Plus, there's something else that I haven't told you."

Gabe raised his eyebrows. "Okay, spill it."

"I think the Shadow Demon is after Tony."

Gabe turned to face him, straddling the log. He glowered at Nick. "The thing that's killing people in Europe? It's here?"

"I think so. Tony told me that something was trying to capture him. It tried to drag him somewhere, but luckily, he escaped. He was scared shitless, though. Can't say as I blame him."

Gabe studied Nick's face for a long moment. "I don't like this one little bit."

"I agree. That's why I want to cross over this ghost as soon as possible."

Gabe gave him a scornful look. "That's not what I meant. You shouldn't be having anything to do with Tony and Tyler if that thing is after them. What if it's using Tony as bait to get to you?"

"Funny you mentioned that," Nick said. "Nate suspected the same thing. But I plan on taking extra precautions tomorrow and doing extra protection rituals. I'll be fine, and I'll call you the moment it's over."

Gabe held his gaze for a moment and laughed.

"What's so funny?" Nick asked.

"You act as though I'm not going to be there, right by your side."

"Gabe, I don't think—"

"Regardless of what you may think, I'm going to be there," Gabe said, cutting him off. "Or did you forget your promise to me?"

Nick knew very well to what promise Gabe was referring—the promise that he'd never enter into a situation involving a ghost without Gabe at his side. But this time, things were different. This time Nick was dealing with a mass-murdering demon. There was no way he could involve Gabe in that.

"Gabe, you don't understand. This thing has killed people. If it shows up, I can't concentrate on getting rid of it and protecting you simultaneously. There's no way I can allow you to get involved in this one."

Gabe's retort came quickly. "And there's no way you can stop me."

"Gabe—"

Gabe poked him in the chest with his index finger. "No, you listen to me for a moment. We're in this together. Time and time again, we've seen that we're stronger together. Maybe I can view the situation from a perspective different from you or see something that you missed."

Nick sighed. "If anything happens to you, your mother will kill me."

"And I'll kill you if you try to do this without me."

They stared at each other for a moment.

Nick cleared his throat dramatically. "Gabe," he said in a low voice. "I haven't even encountered this thing yet, so I don't know what to expect if it does show up. All I know is that it's deadly. It's too dangerous for you to be there. You have no experience in dealing with demons."

Gabe crossed his arms over his chest. "And you do?"

He has a point, Nick thought. "Don't be like this," Nick said. "You need to understand that I'm terrified for your safety. If anything were to happen to you, I'd be like Tyler. I'd never be able to move past it. Never."

Gabe swallowed. "And you think I'd be able to? We need each other. We need to be there to watch each other's back. Nick, I'm not gonna back down on this one. You are *not* crossing over this ghost unless I'm there with you."

Nick sighed in exasperation and threw up his arms. Gabe certainly was relentless. "Fine. But you need to stay back and out of the way, especially if anything weird starts happening."

Gabe chuckled. "Something weird happening with you around? Now that would be a first."

Nick grinned, despite his irritation with Gabe. "Just promise, okay?"

Gabe nodded. "I promise. I'll stay out of the way and let you do your thing. Now, to move onto more important matters."

"Huh?"

Gabe's smile widened. "Here we are, all alone in the woods with nobody for miles." He winked. "Don't you think we should take advantage of this opportunity?"

Nick stared at him, confused. "What opportunity?"

Gabe scuttled closer to Nick and put his hands on Nick's knees. "Do I have to spell it out for y'all?"

Nick locked eyes with Gabe, and his heart started pounding. What did Gabe have in mind? Nick wasn't sure if he was ready yet. He was, but he wasn't. Nick felt a tingle in his stomach, and his mind no longer seemed capable of giving his body commands.

Gabe stood up. "Come here," he said, holding out his hand. Nick took his hand, and Gabe pulled him up. Gabe pointed to the ground underneath a giant pine tree. "Over there."

Gabe pulled him toward the tree and then pulled Nick down on top of him. Nick landed harder than he thought he would.

"Did I hurt you?" Nick asked.

Gabe nuzzled Nick's ear and whispered, "Not a bit."

Gabe grazed his lips along Nick's cheeks, making Nick shudder. Gabe brushed his lips against Nick's neck. Nick whimpered in response.

"You like that, do you?" Gabe whispered.

"Uh-huh." Nick wrapped his arms tighter around Gabe, pulling him closer. His heart was pounding in his chest. He ran his hand up and down Gabe's back and tucked it under the t-shirt Gabe was wearing. Gabe groaned.

Then, in one swift move, Gabe flipped him over so that he was on his back. Gabe straddled him, a devilish smile on his face. Gabe pinned Nick's wrists to the ground, and Nick wiggled underneath him.

Gabe's expression then grew serious as he gazed into Nick's eyes. Nick's heart pounded harder and harder as Gabe brought his face in closer to Nick's. Gabe's sleepy eyes closed, and he expertly tilted his head — and their mouths met — Gabe's warm, moist lips pressing lightly against his. All the muscles in Nick's face—his entire body—went slack as he fell into Gabe's soft kiss. Nick closed his eyes.

He opened his mouth and felt the tentative sweep of Gabe's tongue. Gabe tasted minty, like fresh peppermint. Nick groaned into the kiss. His entire body now ached for Gabe's touch. The kiss continued, with Gabe occasionally stopping to nip at Nick's lips.

Without breaking the kiss, Gabe pulled Nick so that both rested on their sides, facing each other. He ran his fingers through Nick's curly hair with one hand, the other resting on the back of Nick's head, gently guiding him into Gabe's lips.

Once again, Nick slipped his fingers beneath Gabe's shirt, aching for the heat of bare skin. His palm pressed against Gabe's back, gliding slowly up and down the length of his spine. Gabe's body burned under his touch. A soft sigh escaped Gabe, and he drew Nick closer, clutching him tighter in the embrace.

Through Gabe's thin shirt, Nick felt the firm muscles of his shoulders and chest. Gabe's arms wrapped around him, and Nick melted into the embrace, surrendering completely. Gabe was unraveling his sanity with nothing but his mouth.

Slowly, Gabe pulled back, their lips parting, and then brushed their cheeks together. Nick squirmed, startled by the rasp of Gabe's light stubble grazing his skin.

Nick looked up. Gabe's disheveled blond hair was damp with sweat, and Nick could feel his hardness pressed against his own. Gabe smiled, lowered his head, and let his lips wander across Nick's face.

"I've been waiting to get you alone for a while," he said, his voice deep and throaty.

Nick nodded, feeling helpless against Gabe's twinkling smile. "Me too," was all he could manage to say.

Eyes still glued to Nick, he slid his hands under Nick's shirt and ran his hands up and down Nick's chest. A tingle ran up and down his spine in time to Gabe's hand movements. "Is it okay if I do this?"

"Uh-huh." The squeak of Nick's voice surprised him.

Gabe gave Nick a broad smile. "You're a really good kisser."

"So are you," said Nick, his voice sounding more normal now. "It gets better every time."

"They say practice makes perfect."

Nick's hardness still throbbed against his jeans. Even the sound of Gabe's voice was sending him over the edge. Nick glanced at the quickly darkening sky. "We probably should be going," he said softly, without conviction. "It's starting to get late, and my mom will have a shit-fit if I miss dinner. I wish we—"

"What time is it?" asked Gabe.

Nick grabbed his phone from the nightstand and glanced at the screen. "Almost 6:00."

"You're right. It is getting late." The pained look on Gabe's face told Nick that he was disappointed. Had Gabe expected something more? Was Nick wrong to put a halt to it? *Congratulations Michelson. You screwed it up again.*

Gabe grabbed hold of Nick's hand. "It's fine."

Nick met Gabe's stare. "What?"

Gabe swallowed. "Stopping. Now. It's okay."

What, was Gabe a friggin' mind reader now?

"You sure? I didn't mean to... "

"This isn't the right place, and now's not the right time. And you're right. It'll be dark soon. We don't want to end up being bear food, now do we?"

Gabe started to his feet.

"Wait," said Nick.

"How about next weekend?" Nick almost choked on the question.

"Next weekend?"

Nick nodded. "My mom said I could stay here overnight on the weekends if I wanted to. I haven't yet. I don't like the idea of being here by myself." He paused and swallowed. "But maybe you can stay here with me?"

Nick felt his heart pick up speed as he waited for Gabe's response.

Gabe showed Nick his devilish smile and brought his hand to Nick's cheek. "You sure about this?"

Nick stared at him for a long moment. "Yeah," he said in a whisper.

"I mean really, really, truly sure?"

Nick nodded. "I think so."

"You think so?"

"I mean, yes. Definitely. I'm sure," said Nick. "I'm just a little nervous."

"And you think I'm not?"

Nick met Gabe's gaze, and they both broke out into a grin. "Next weekend, then," Nick said. "It's a date."

The smile on Gabe's face told Nick that he had said the right thing.

CHAPTER TEN

"DINNER WAS EXCELLENT, LIZ, AS USUAL," said Nick's father, pushing his plate to the side. "Chicken with Apples, always one of my favorites. Did you add extra pepper? I loved the extra zing to it."

Nick nodded in agreement, one last forkful of food still in his mouth. As usual, he was the last one eating. When finished, Nick tossed his fork and knife onto the plate, making a loud clang. His mother shot him a look that Nick pretended he didn't see. He laid his napkin on the table.

His mother pointed to Nick's sister. "I do believe it's your turn to do the washing up."

"No way! It's Nick's turn."

"Sorry, Missy, but I cleaned up last night," Nick said. "You're it."

"Can't you do it tonight?" asked Melissa, glaring at her mother. "I have a ton of homework I have to do."

His mother let go of a long, exaggerated sigh. "Why on earth do we have to go through this every single time it's your turn?"

"But it's not—"

"No. You are not wiggling out of it again. Everyone does their chores without complaining. Everyone except for you, that is. I'm not letting you off the hook this time, young lady." She pointed to the kitchen. "March."

Melissa rolled her eyes, harrumphed, and let go with a dramatic, long drawn-out sigh. In almost slow motion, she rose and began gathering up the plates, grunting each time she picked up a dish as though she were lifting giant boulders instead of dinner plates. Just as she snatched up Nick's plate, an intense stomach cramp hit him hard, causing him to rear back in his chair. His skin rose in goosebumps. His father's eyes grew wide.

"Nick, what is it? Are you alright?" his father asked.

Nick nodded and was just about to respond when Tony appeared, standing right behind his mother.

"Well?" asked Tony. "Did you talk to him? Is he willing to meet me?"

This was precisely what Nick was afraid of—that ghosts would pop in unannounced in the middle of the living room while his entire family was present.

Nick felt his father's eyes glued to him. Nick nodded.

"Yes? When?"

"Tomorrow after school," Nick said, in as low a voice as he could.

"What's going on tomorrow after school?" Nick's mother asked.

"Nothing."

She creased her brow. "But you said something about tomorrow after school."

Melissa stood in the middle of the room, holding a pile of dishes and staring at Nick.

"Missy, I need you to get in the kitchen," his father said.

"I'm going, I'm going," she said but didn't move.

"Now," said their father.

"Alright, I'm going." She left the room, shuffling her feet as she did so.

Nick raised his eyes to meet Tony's. "He'll be there at 4:30. I didn't tell him about you crossing over."

His mother glared at him. "Nick, what on earth are you..." Her expression then changed, informing Nick that she had figured out what's going on.

"At the cabin, then?" asked Tony. He had a massive grin on his face.

"Yes. He'll be meeting us at the cabin."

Tony nodded once, smiled, and then was gone.

"I'm sorry about that," Nick said. His voice trembled as he spoke, and his throat jutted with a hard swallow. He glanced once toward the kitchen to make sure Missy wasn't listening. As of yet, she knew nothing at all about Nick's abilities.

"So there was a..." his mother paused, as if looking for the right word. "A spirit here? In this room?"

Nick nodded. "They usually never do that. Appear here like that, I mean.... well, almost never."

The sound of clattering dishes rang from the kitchen. His mother's expression grew stern. "You need to tell them not to come here again, especially when your family is around."

"I'll tell him. I promise."

"So what was that all about?" she asked. "Who's meeting you at the cabin?"

"There's a ghost of a kid at school who wants to talk to his best friend before he crosses over. I promised that I'd arrange a final meeting for them." The lie came out of Nick's mouth before he could stop it. He didn't want to tell his parents the truth-that the ghost was gay and wanted to talk to his boyfriend. He didn't know how his parents would react to that—and this was a door that Nick wasn't quite ready to open yet. Soon perhaps, but not now.

Nick glanced over and met his father's eyes. He could tell from the expression on his face that his father didn't believe him. "Are you sure it's safe to be alone with this..." His father lowered his voice. "This person?"

"I've spoken with him a couple of times already, and he seems okay. I've dealt with much scarier ghosts than him before."

"Nick, keep your voice down," said his mother. She gestured to the kitchen with her head.

"Oh, right. Sorry."

"I just don't think Melissa's ready yet to learn about your abilities," his mother said. "We should wait until she's a little older."

"Agreed," said Nick.

Nick slid his chair back and rose. His father put a hand on his arm.

"As always, Nick, be careful. You might not always know what a ghost's true intentions are."

Wow. He actually said the word ghost. Points for him. "I'll be happy once this one crosses over," Nick said. "He's been kind of challenging."

His father gave him a brief nod. "I imagine they all are, in their own way. Good luck."

~

"HELLO?" called out Nick. He was early, but had no idea whether Tony would arrive before him. He was surprised he'd managed to convince Tyler to come. Tyler hadn't been the most receptive to much of anything Nick had said in the past, but when Nick told him that Tony wanted to speak through him, Tyler readily agreed. He hated lying to the kid, but if that was the only way to get Tony to cross over, then so be it. However, Nick didn't consider it to be *lying* exactly—he simply neglected to tell Tyler that the reason they were getting together was so that Tony could say one last goodbye before he crossed over.

Nick sat on the couch and waited, unsure of why he felt so nervous. He wondered if his uncle would approve of him inviting a ghost to his house, though it wasn't his uncle's house anymore. It was Nick's. Still, a rogue thought tapped his brain, whispering to him that something was not right with this meeting. Ah yes, the protections! He'd almost forgotten to do them, and that wouldn't have been a good thing.

Nick bolted up and hurriedly did the rituals that Katrina had shown him, rituals that supposedly banished and denied entry to any being whose intentions did not reside in the light. In other words, no big bad boogeymen could get in—or at least he hoped.

When he'd finished, he looked around the room and took a deep breath. He'd lit a couple of white taper candles for atmosphere, and the room was in perfect order. He'd considered burning incense too, but thought better of it. What if Tyler didn't like the fragrance, or worse yet, was allergic to it? Then all the evening's planning would have been for naught. Even though Katrina often had incense burning in her store, she never lit it when clients were scheduled unless they specifically requested it.

Nick stood up and walked again to the window. He shouldn't have gotten here so early. He hated waiting—it was one of the things that Nick despised the most. It was rare that he'd wait in a line for anything. His mother called it a bad case of impatience, but to Nick, waiting was a waste of time—time he could spend doing more constructive things.

He eyed his Tarot deck on the table and wondered if its presence would bother Tyler. Hell, it shouldn't, given that his boyfriend was a ghost, and they were all meeting here this evening to have a conversation with said ghost. Nick considered throwing down a few cards to see how the evening's events would transpire when a light knocking at the door interrupted his thoughts. Must be Tyler—he doubted if Tony would come in via the front door. He was worried that Tyler would get lost, as the cabin was a bit tricky to find.

Nick opened the door and blinked in surprise when he saw both Tony and Tyler standing on the step.

"What?" said Tyler.

"I should have figured that you'd both arrive together," Nick said, locking gazes with Tony.

"Tony's here? With me?"

Nick nodded and gestured with his hand for them to enter the cabin. "Come in."

Tyler gazed around the room. "Nice. So this is your own place?"

"Yes, and no. I inherited it from my uncle, but I'm not allowed to stay here full time. Only on weekends."

"Sweet!" Tyler said. "How awesome to have your very own digs. I would have loved to have had my own cabin or house with Tony."

Before he could respond, Tony interrupted. "Can we get started?"

Nick gave him a curt nod. "Tony's ready to speak to you now."

Tyler widened his eyes. "What do I have to do? Do I need to concentrate or anything?"

"Nope, nothing. I'll tell you what Tony says." Nick gestured to the light purple couch against the wall. "You can sit down, though. It'd be more comfortable."

"Oh, right," said Tyler. He took a seat on the couch, and Nick plopped down next to him. Tony sat in the dark green stuffed chair across from the sofa.

"Where is he?" Tyler asked.

"In the chair directly across from us," Nick said.

"Tell him that I miss him, and I'm so glad to see him," said Tony.

"Tony says that he misses you and he's happy to see you. He's glad that you agreed to meet him like this."

"How could I refuse? Oh, Tony, it's so hard with you gone."

"It's hard for me too, Ty," said Tony. "Not being able to touch you like we used to do."

Nick repeated what the ghost had said.

"But I'm here now," said Tony.

Nick creased his brow and repeated Tony's words.

Tyler swallowed and nodded. "I feel better knowing that you're at least around me. It was so lonely thinking you were gone forever."

"Don't you worry, babe. I'm not going anywhere."

What in the hell is he doing? "Tony?" said Nick.

Tony held up his index finger in a wait-a-moment gesture. "Just let me talk to him like this for a minute."

"Just for a minute," Nick said.

"What's he saying?" asked Tyler.

"He told you not to worry, that he'll always be around."

Tyler smiled. "I wish I could see you. It strange talking to you when you're invisible."

"I imagine. So who was it that you took to the prom?"

"He wants to know who you took to the prom."

"Jealous?" Tyler chuckled. "I took my friend, Ginny, only because she pestered me half to death. I would never have gone otherwise. It was you who I wanted to go with."

"And I would have gladly gone with you. Did you have a good time?"

Nick repeated what the ghost said.

"Not really. I was missing you too badly."

"I was right there with you," said Tony.

"He said that he was right there with you," Nick said. "And I can vouch for that. The prom was the first time I met him."

"I wish I would have known at the time. Maybe we could have had a dance together. Although I suppose it would have looked kind of weird to other people."

Tony chuckled. "I suppose it would have. But no matter. We can have all the private dances we want."

Oh crap. That didn't sound promising. "Do you think it's wise to get his hopes up like that?" Nick asked.

"What are you saying?" asked Tyler.

"Your role is to help me talk to Tyler," said Tony. "As we agreed."

"No," said Nick. "That wasn't the deal. I'm here to help you say *goodbye*—so you can finally move on."

"Cross over?" asked Tyler. "Tony, you can't! Don't leave me."

"Don't you worry about that, Ty. I'm not going anywhere. I'll always be with you."

Nick felt anger rise within him like acidic bile. "You never planned on crossing over, did you?"

Tony glared at him but said nothing.

"You friggin' used me," said Nick as realization dawned. "That's low, dude."

"How dare you judge me?" said Tony. "You see how he is, how lost he is without me. He needs me."

Nick crossed his arms in front of his chest. "The only reason he's lost is because you can't let go."

"What's going on?" interrupted Tyler. "Is he leaving?"

Nick snapped his head to Tony. "Good question. So what is it? Are you leaving?"

"No."

Nick closed his eyes, trying to keep his anger in check. He'd been duped by a bloody ghost.

"No," said Nick. "He's not leaving. At least not right now."

Tyler let go of a long sigh of apparent relief and nodded. "Promise you'll never leave me."

Tony appeared next to Tyler on the couch. He kissed him on the cheek. "I promise."

"What did he say?" asked Tyler.

Nick knew he shouldn't be angry with Tyler. It wasn't his fault. "He said he promises."

"Tell him that I love him and that he never has to worry. I'm watching over him."

Nick repeated Tony's words.

"And tell him—"

"No," said Nick, crossing his arms over his chest. "No more. I'm done. You told me to get Tyler here so you can say goodbye before you cross over. It's obvious that you don't have any intentions of doing that. So this meeting is over."

Tony scowled, reached over and flung the coffee table over on its side. Tyler and Nick gasped in unison.

"What about you helping people?" the ghost screamed at him. He sneered. "Isn't that what you said you do? Or was that one big lie? You are the only way that I can talk to Tyler. What's the big deal in helping us every now and then? Huh?"

"This is wrong, Tony, and I think you know it," said Nick, trying to keep the calm in his voice. He stood up and righted the table, hoping they wouldn't notice how much his hands were trembling. "You need to cross over into the light, where you belong. Hanging on to Tyler this way is unhealthy for the both of you."

Tyler stood up abruptly and pointed an index finger at Nick. "And who in the fuck are you to decide what's best for me? Tony is what's best for me. I love him, and he loves me. What's so wrong with that?"

Nick opened his mouth to respond when all at once, a gust of wind shook the cabin. The front door blew wide open, and the magazines that were on the floor flew about the room. Nick turned to Tony, but he was gone.

"Tyler," said Nick, but he was already walking to the door.

"Skip it," Tyler said, without looking back. He walked through the doorway, and the door slammed behind him.

"Asshole!" Nick yelled, looking up at the ceiling, but he knew that nobody had heard him. The ghost had already left.

CHAPTER ELEVEN

"Do you want me and your father to come with you?" Nick's mother asked. She sat at the dining room table and had been quietly working on the computer until Nick told her where he was going.

"No. I'd rather go alone."

"Are you sure you're ready?" she asked. "It hasn't been all that long. It might be better if someone goes with you. Maybe we could pay a visit to Grandma's grave while we're there."

"Next time," said Nick. "I promise." Even though Nick hoped with all his being and wanted more than anything to believe that his uncle had crossed over when he died, Nick wanted to try to make contact. Just in case he was still hanging around—or worse, trapped by the Shadow Demon, as both he and Katrina suspected.

She took a deep breath. "I understand." She paused and studied his face. "Remember, honey, you can always come to your father or me if you ever need to talk about anything. You do know that, right?"

"Thanks, Mom," Nick said. "I will." This was something,

however, that he did not want to talk over with his parents. What would he even say? That he was hoping to speak with his dead uncle in an attempt to find out whether an evil demon had him trapped? While his parents were trying their damnedest to be open-minded about his abilities, he knew that there was only so much they would understand. Talking about demons would definitely be crossing a line. That, and he didn't want them to think he was in any danger.

Nick arrived at the cemetery twenty minutes later and breathed a sigh of relief when he saw that the place was deserted. He didn't want anyone thinking he was crazy—though he supposed that it's not all that unusual for someone to be talking out loud at the grave of a loved one. He'd seen people do it before when he'd visited graves of relatives with his parents. A moment later, after he got out of the car, he heard a lawnmower start up. So the place wasn't deserted after all. Nick turned his head toward the loud noise and noticed a skinny kid who looked a couple of years younger than Nick pushing a bright red mower around a grave. Nick was glad that he was on the opposite side of the cemetery.

He found his uncle's headstone with little difficulty, as his father had given him good instructions. He swallowed when he saw the shiny tall brown tombstone: Mitchell Alan Michelson. Seeing it in stone made it so final.

"Uncle Mitch?" Nick said out loud. "Are you around? Katrina and I are worried about you."

He waited. Nothing.

He then had a thought. None of the ghosts he'd ever encountered had been at the cemetery. Apparently, ghosts hang around the living, not the dead. Still, he pressed on.

"There's been some dark entity of some kind snatching

spirits as they're about to cross over," Nick continued. "I just want to know that you're okay and that you made it across."

He paused, not quite sure where he was going with this. Might as well go for the cliché. "If you can give me a sign of some sort that you're safe, I'd appreciate it. Also, I have a stubborn ghost here that won't cross over. So if you have any ideas, I'd love some advice."

Nick closed his eyes and waited. Still nothing. A soft, warm breeze blew across his face, but there were no messages from the Other Side. No stomach flips. No goosebumps. No messages from his uncle.

The slamming of a car door snapped him out of his concentration. A familiar figure stood at a gravesite not too far from where Nick was standing.

It was Tyler Tarrant.

Nick hesitated for a moment and then slowly walked toward Tyler. As Nick got closer, he could hear Tyler talking, apparently to Tony.

"I don't know if you can hear me, Tony, but I wanted to say how sorry I am. I was going to tell you that the other night when we were with that Nick kid, but I didn't get the chance. So hopefully, you're listening now. What I want to tell you, is that I can't help but feel that your death is my fault. If I had gone swimming with you that day, this wouldn't have happened." Tyler was obviously sobbing now, and he struggled to get his words out. "I wish I hadn't believed that whatever I had to do that day was more important than going with you for a swim. You wouldn't have drowned if I'd been with you because I would have been there to save you." He swallowed and wiped his eyes with his sleeve. "Oh Tony, I'm so sorry. I'm sorry I didn't go with you when you asked, and I'm sorry you died there alone."

Nick took a deep breath and cleared his throat. He

didn't want Tyler to think he was deliberately eavesdropping, even though he was.

Tyler looked up, and his eyes widened. "You again. What in the fuck are you doing here? Are you stalking me or something?"

Nick held up both of his hands, palms out. "Whoa, dude. Chill. I'm here visiting my uncle's grave, and I noticed you over here. I wanted to come over and apologize."

"Oh, sorry." He sucked in a deep breath as though trying to compose himself. "When did your uncle die?"

"A few months back. It's all still pretty fresh, you know?"

"Believe me, I know," said Tyler. "And it doesn't seem to get any easier."

"Tell me about it."

"So you and your uncle were tight?"

"Very. He was more like my best friend than my uncle."

"I'm sorry for your loss."

"So about the other night," Nick said, changing the subject. "I felt bad that things ended the way they did. It's just that Tony told me that the reason he wanted you there was to say goodbye. He led me to believe that he was ready to cross over."

Tyler frowned and looked at Nick sharply. "So you deliberately deceived me? Lied to me?"

"It wasn't me," Nick tried to explain. "Tony made me promise not to tell you that he was going to leave. He didn't think you'd come otherwise."

His frown deepened. "He would have been right."

"It's not you who was deceived Tyler, it was me. It's clear now that Tony never had any intentions of going. Instead, he orchestrated our meeting simply so he could chat with you."

"And what's so wrong with that?" Tyler said. His eyes

blazed cold. "What's so wrong with wanting to communicate with each other? You have no idea how hard it's been."

"Actually, I do. I recently lost not only my uncle but also my grandmother, both only a few weeks apart."

"It's not the same thing," Tyler answered in a hoarse whisper. "He was the love of my life."

Nick stood silently for a moment, desperately attempting to retain his composure and gather his thoughts. "I didn't mean to trivialize your relationship with Tony. I'm only saying that I know how hard it is to lose people you love and how difficult it is to let them go."

"And why should I let him go? Tony's here with me." His eyes widened. "Would you be willing to help me communicate again with Tony? Not all the time—maybe every now and then?"

"I don't think that's a good idea," said Nick. Then, seeing Tyler's angry expression, he added, "It's not healthy to make him the center of your life. He's supposed to move on to the next stage of his journey, whatever that might be, and you're supposed to live your life. You're supposed to—"

"Just fucking forget it," Tyler interrupted with sudden fury. He turned to leave, but Nick grabbed his arm.

"Tyler, please."

Tyler stopped in his tracks and shook loose from Nick's grasp. "What? You're just being an asshole for refusing to help me. I thought you said that you help people, that it's what you do. You're just a liar and a freak."

Tyler's words stung. "Believe what you want to of me," Nick said. "But you have to think about what's best for Tony. He's trapped here without a body, without being able to see anyone or talk to anyone. It's not fair to him. He needs to move on."

Tyler studied Nick's face for a long moment. He shrugged. "I dunno. Maybe you're right."

"Will you at least think about it? At least think about helping me to get Tony to move on."

Tyler stayed deathly still and stared at Nick, expressionless. Finally, he let go of a lengthy sigh, his breath now visible in the cool evening air.

"I'll think about it."

With that, he turned and walked away. Nick thought it best not to go after him. But, at least he agreed to think about it.

"I know you're here, Tony," said Nick. "I've felt you since the moment I started talking to Tyler."

Tony appeared in front of Nick and sat on his own tombstone, which Nick thought was kind of creepy. Tony stared intently at Nick.

"Then why didn't you say something earlier?" Tony asked.

"Because this was between Tyler and me." Nick sighed. "So I suppose you're going to tell me that I'm wrong for what I told him?"

Tony slowly shook his head. "I know you're right. I'm just worried about him, about how he'll manage without me. You know?"

Nick stared at him for a long moment and nodded. "But there comes a point where you have to let him go. He has a future to plan for." Although Nick should be one to talk—he's not finding it very easy to let go of his uncle. "I take it you heard Tony's apology?"

"I heard it. He's completely wrong to feel guilty about anything. I had no idea. This was not his fault in the least." He paused, looked down at the ground for a moment, and then turned his regard back to Nick. "But there's more that he doesn't know."

Nick raised his eyebrows. "Oh?"

"While Tyler was talking, I started remembering bits and pieces of what happened that day. I told you that I remembered someone else being with me that day. I still can't recall any of the details, just random flashes. Those are still elusive. But I remember one thing for absolute certain. I wasn't alone that day."

A shiver rattled through Nick. "This changes things, especially given that your body was discovered by a local the next day."

Tony ignored him. "While Tyler was talking, I remembered calling him and asking him if he wanted to go for a swim. I didn't want to go alone—because that would have been boring. So I ended up going to Doctor's Park with someone else that day."

"Who was it? Someone you know?"

"That's the kicker," said Tony, locking his gaze on Nick. "I still have no idea. For the life of me, I can't remember who it was. It's maddening as hell."

Nick swallowed. "Do you think that this person might have had something to do with your death?"

Tony straightened, and a look of surprise crossed over his expression. "The thought hadn't occurred to me. I've been so occupied with trying to remember who was with me that I never even considered that someone might have killed me." He stewed on Nick's words for a moment, then shook his head. "But no. I drowned. I'm sure of it."

"Are you absolutely positive about that?"

"Absolutely? Yes. Well...mostly. I remember there was water in my mouth, my nose, my throat, and I recall not being able to breathe." He studied Nick's face. "Why do you think this person might have had something to do with my death? Do you know something I don't?"

"According to what I've read, your body wasn't found until the day after you drowned. If there *was* someone with you, why didn't they notify anyone? Wouldn't they have called someone? Like an ambulance? Or the police?"

Tony heaved himself to his feet, although he hovered about a half an inch from the ground. "You're right! If there was someone with me, why didn't they call someone?" He stared at Nick. "Or why didn't they try to save me?"

"Tony, you've got to try to remember. This might be why you're still here, why you haven't crossed over."

"That is not the reason," Tony protested. He glared at Nick. "I'm here because of Tyler. I can't leave him. Not yet."

Nick held up both his hands. "No need to get pissed off. I'm just tossing out ideas. I'm only trying to help."

Tony's face softened. "I get that. This is just so damned frustrating, not being able to remember." He blinked. "But you'll help me, won't you? I need to find out who was there that day."

"What is it that you want me to do?"

Tony considered this. "Don't tell Tyler that there was someone with me."

Nick creased his brow. "Huh? Not that Tyler is all that receptive to talking to me, but even if he was, why not tell him? Don't you think he'd want to know?"

"I don't want him to know. So let's keep this between you and me for now."

"Okay, Tony, what's really going on here? There's something you're not telling me."

"There isn't."

"You're lying," said Nick.

His well-rehearsed demeanor crumbled. "I'm telling the

truth. I'm not lying. It's just that," he hesitated and closed his eyes for a moment. "What if I was cheating on Tyler? What if I was fucking around with someone else, and I just can't remember? I'd never want Tyler to know about it. God, that would kill him. I want his memories of me to be good ones, not ugly ones."

Nick eyed Tony carefully. "Did you cheat on Tyler while you were dating, that you remember?"

"No, never! I'd never do anything to hurt Tyler."

Nick creased his brow. "Then what makes you think you were cheating on him that day with someone else?"

"Because whoever was there with me didn't come forward. Maybe he knows Tyler? Knows the both of us? The only thing that makes any kind of sense was that I was with someone who didn't want anyone else to know."

The breeze had picked up even more now, causing Nick to shiver continuously. "Before we jump to any more conclusions, let's see if we can figure this out. Okay?"

Tony nodded. "But you won't tell Tyler?"

Nick shook his head. "No, for the moment. But you've got to try to work some more on your memory." Nick tapped his chin. "Have you been to the park since the accident?"

Tony flashed him a panicked look. "You mean the place where I died?"

Nick nodded. "Maybe going back there might trigger some memories."

Tony slowly shook his head. "I haven't been back. I figured it'd be tacky to revisit where I died. Tacky and creepy."

"Would you be willing to give it a try? I'd go there with you if you like."

Tony hesitated. "If the memories don't come back to me,

then yes. We can go to the park. But not quite yet, okay? I'm not ready."

"Understood. I'm not gonna force you to do anything. I can't imagine how difficult that would be."

"I need you to talk to Tyler again."

Nick raised his eyebrows. "Because it went so well the last time I talked to him."

"You need to prepare him if I do decide to leave."

"How do I know I can trust you?"

The ghost reared back. "What do you mean?"

"Come on, Tony. The last time you deceived me and made me look like an idiot. Yeah, I'm not going to allow you to take advantage of me like that again."

"I was wrong. I'm sorry. But you certainly can understand that I only did it so I could talk to Tyler? It's been so frustrating not being able to communicate with him—or anyone else, for that matter. Well, except for you."

"I get that. But that still doesn't excuse how you treated me." Nick sighed. "I'll do it, I suppose. In the meantime, you can work on figuring out who was with you."

Tony nodded, and, without saying anything further, vanished.

"YOU'RE OFF THE HOOK TODAY," said Katrina. Her head of huge red hair looked even wilder today than usual. "Your 4:30 canceled."

"Yay!" said Nick and reached for his coat, which he had only hung up two minutes prior.

"Don't sound so happy, Nicholas," she said, looking over her reading glasses. "A cancellation means no money for you nor for me."

"I know," said Nick, trying to suppress a smile. He had two quizzes coming up, neither of which he'd been able to study for very much. This Tyler and Tony situation had taken up too much of his valuable study time.

"You can stay for a lesson if you like," said Katrina.

Nick shook his head. "Not today. I have a boatload of studying to do."

"Fair enough. Speaking of lessons, have you been working on your protection exercises? And using them every time you leave the house?"

"I have... for the most part."

She closed her eyes and shook her head. "There should not be any exceptions to this. This needs to become a habit that's so automatic that you do it without even thinking. You know how important this is."

"I've been pretty good at remembering, but—"

She took his hands, silencing him. "There are no buts. This is absolutely essential. I don't need to remind you that some creature is murdering your fellow mediums."

"Believe me, I don't need reminding. That demon thing has been on my mind pretty much constantly. I promise I'll be better and will never leave the house without doing those protections visualizations."

She patted the top of his hands. "I'd feel better knowing that. Speaking of, have you heard from our French friend as of late?"

Nick shook his head. "Not since the last time he called me in person. The big psychic convention is this week, I think. Or was it next week? Regardless, Nate said he'd contact me afterward to let me know what they discussed and decided."

"How about your ghost friend—what was his name? Tyler?"

"No, Tyler's the boyfriend. The ghost's name is Tony."

"Ah, yes. Have you seen him recently?"

"Um..."

"Don't forget Nicholas, I know if you're lying to me." She tapped on her forehead. "Psychic, remember?"

Nick's eyes widened. "You can really tell when I lie?"

She chuckled. "If you mean can I always divine when you're stretching the truth, the answer is no. I can, however, usually tell from your mannerisms. You're not a very good liar, Nicholas Michelson."

"Oh," he said and breathed a sigh of relief, happy that Katrina wasn't reading his mind. "Yeah, my parents have always been able to tell when I'm not quite telling them the entire truth."

"So this Tony. Has he had any additional contact with the Shadow Demon?"

He rested his jacket down on the counter and stuffed his hands into his pockets. "Not that he's mentioned. The sooner I can cross this ghost over, the better I'll feel, and I can stop worrying about anything trying to attack him again."

"Unless this demon was only using the ghost to get to you, as Nate suggested." She sucked in a deep breath. "The more I think about it, the more I wish you'd consider simply walking away from this one. As much as I disapprove of this relationship between a ghost and a human, it's dangerous for you to be involved right now."

Nick closed his eyes briefly, then reopened them. "I know. But I also know that my uncle would never walk away from helping someone, and neither can I. I started this, and now I need to finish it. I can't let those two continue like that. They both deserve to get on with their lives, as you said earlier."

She smiled, although sadly. "I completely understand, but I can't help but worry."

He nodded briefly, without meeting her eyes. "I'll be fine. Really. I'll double-up on my protection rituals and keep my eyes open for anything strange."

Nick saw her shiver. "I suppose that's all I can ask. Good lord, I hope those European psychics can figure out what this thing is and how to get rid of it. Think of all the poor souls that are not crossing over because mediums have been killed. There so few of them—of you—that the world cannot spare additional losses." She gently touched his arm. "Nor can those of us who love them."

Nick's jaw tightened, and he nodded without responding. He snatched his jacket from the counter and put it on.

"Don't forget you have a reading tomorrow," Katrina said.

"I do? I don't think I have that on my calendar."

"It's with someone named Marc. He specifically requested a male reader." She narrowed her eyes. "I apologize if I neglected to tell you. I thought I texted you last night."

Nick creased his brow. He pulled out his phone, and sure enough, there was a text from Katrina and one from Gabe. He'd forgotten to turn off airplane mode on his phone.

"Sorry. I had my phone turned off. I'll be here tomorrow at..." he glanced at his phone again. "4:45."

They said their goodbyes, and Nick was out the door. He'd begun walking toward his mom's car when he noticed a young man across the street. The young man was looking right at Nick, and then, before he could meet Nick's gaze, he immediately looked away. Strange. It seems that every time he goes out, he sees the same guy who always seems to be staring at him. Nick didn't think he was a ghost, given that he didn't receive any of the usual physical warnings when there was a ghost nearby. Nick looked away and, on a whim, stopped off at Kyle's Comics to see if there were any recent issues of his favorite comics.

Having left the store empty-handed, he noticed a nervous, fidgety middle-aged man standing by the lamp store. As Nick passed him, his stomach lurched. Now, this guy was a ghost. Nick made a point of not making eye contact with the man, not wanting to let him know that Nick could see him.

"Are you the one?" he asked Nick, just as Nick was about to pass him by. So much for appearing inconspicuous.

"I beg your pardon?" Nick said automatically. Dammit!

"You are him!" the man exclaimed. "I knew it. Thank goodness."

"Do we know each other?"

The man shook his head. "Not yet. But I've heard all about you."

Nick looked around him to ensure that there wasn't anyone overhearing their conversation. He gestured to the man to join him under the awning that hung over the lamp store. Nick faced the window.

"How have you heard about me?" Nick asked. "From whom?"

"Let me tell you, my boy, you've made some powerful enemies. Yes, indeed. There are some who are not at all happy with what you've been doing. Not in the least."

Nick glanced away from the man and took a step back. Shit! He'd forgotten to do his protection rituals. What if this man is the murderer of psychics that everyone is talking about? Should he try and run? What would be his chances of getting away?

"Who are you?" Nick asked, returning his gaze to the spirit.

"Oh, sorry." The man bowed reverently. "Charlie English, at your service."

Nick suppressed a chuckle at the man's overly formal way of talking. "So you know me? How?"

The man looked over his shoulder warily. "You're a hot topic of conversation among souls who are still hanging around here. You're the fellow to go to for help. They call you the Light One."

Nick snorted. "The Light One? You're kidding me, right?"

The man creased his brow. "Now, why would I be kidding?"

Nick shrugged. "I didn't think any ghosts knew who I was. I try to keep a low profile."

"A low profile?" The man covered his mouth with his hand and chuckled. "Oh, that's a good one. You're funny."

"I'm being serious."

"Oh. Sorry." The man looked over his shoulder again, his gaze darting wildly back and forth.

"Why do you keep doing that?" asked Nick. "Are you expecting someone?"

"Good lord, I hope not," said the man in a harsh and distant voice. "I've probably stayed here too long as it is. Must keep on the move. Otherwise, he'll find me."

"Who?" asked Nick, still wary of the stranger, although Nick didn't feel any danger coming from the man. "Who'll find you."

"*Him*."

"That's not much help."

"That's how everyone refers to him—as *Him*, though

some call him as *The One Who Doesn't Belong*. Although he does have a name."

"You're not making much sense, Charlie," Nick said.

"The unholy one. That's also what some ghosts call him. He's unnatural...wrong. He does have a name, though." Charlie leaned forward and whispered in Nick's ear, so quietly that Nick could barely hear him. "Leo."

"Who's Leo?"

"Shhh," said Charlie. "For God sakes, boy, don't call out his name. I don't want him to find me again."

"Okay, dude, this has gone on long enough. Would you tell me who in the fuck this Unholy One is?"

"Such language!"

"Charlie—"

The ghost held up both his hands. "Okay. He's a...well, I'm not exactly sure what he is. I know he was alive at one time—at least, I think he was. That's what they say, anyway. But he's not like the rest of us. He's strong and powerful. I don't know how long he held me for, but I think it was a long time. Months? Years? Who knows. I only recently managed to get away. He's a trapper of souls, is what he is. The guardian of the wretched."

This dude is one major drama queen, thought Nick. "So this Unholy One. You were his prisoner?"

He nodded. "After I died, I saw the light. It was the most beautiful thing I've ever seen. I wanted to cross over into it. But I was fearful. I wasn't always the nicest person in my life, you see. What if I ended up in hell or some other place of torment? So I hesitated—just for a moment. Then he was there. A loud, whirling cyclone of shadows erupted, and he appeared. He grabbed me before I even knew what was happening."

Nick felt his heart race in his chest. *The Shadow Demon.*

"How did you escape?"

"I'm not entirely sure. It's like I was a part of him, absorbed into him somehow. He once said that our souls give him power in the physical. One day, all at once, I felt this strength I didn't know I had. I'd been reflecting on my life, thinking about my wonderful wife, when I felt a surge of power. It was the strangest thing. Extraordinary, actually, now that I think about it. So, using all the energy that I could muster up, I concentrated on escaping. And then whoosh—I was away from him. I was free."

"What can you tell me about him?"

The man leaned in again toward Nick's ear. "He's evil. Pure evil. That's why they call him that name."

"And there are others with him?"

The man nodded rapidly. "Many. Some are trapped, some work with him. He tries to convince some souls to join him and promises them immense power and a place back in the physical world. Some join him; most refuse—or should I say, try to refuse. There's an incredible amount of darkness coming from him." He shook his head. "Just being around him sucks all the joy right out of you. It's the oddest thing."

"So he said he was alive once. So he's a spirit."

"Yes, and no. He was human once, but I'd say he's much more than a spirit. He has such power—power that I've seen no other soul wield."

"Do you know what he wants?"

"Other than power? Not really. I wasn't in his inner circle, so I was not privy to his plans. But I know he's planning something big." He pointed at Nick. "But he's mentioned you."

Nick felt the breath leave his body. "Me?"

"Yes. The Light One. He wants you and has made it his goal to find you and dispose of you. That's why I was looking for you. To warn you about him. You've helped spirits that were supposedly his—or at least according to him. I've also heard him tell the others that if he could trap The Light One, then his power would be complete, that he'd be totally unstoppable." He locked eyes with Nick. "So naturally, you mustn't let that happen."

"I know about him," said Nick. "Or at least I've heard of him. So what does he look like? Like a shadow?"

"Sometimes. But he mostly takes on the form of a young man, not much older looking than you. I guess that must have been what he looked like when he was still alive. It's funny, really. He looks like an unassuming teenager in his physical form—innocent and even trustworthy-looking. I guess that's one of the things that makes him especially dangerous, and one of the reasons he's so successful at tricking and subsequently trapping people."

"Let me get this straight. He looks like a young dude?"

The man nodded. "Mostly. Although I've heard he can take on other forms. Some have speculated that he's lived more than one human life. How, I don't know. Hell, he's almost human now, as he can appear quite physical when he chooses. Those who are not deceased can even see him, unlike most of us."

Nick hesitated, then blurted out the question that had been plaguing him. "Do you know my uncle? His name is Mitchell Michelson. Have you by any chance seen him?"

The man creased his brow in thought. "Not that I can remember. I really didn't know anyone's name, come to think of it. Those of us who he'd trapped were mostly in this horrid state between consciousness and nightmares. There wasn't a whole lot of conversing going on."

"Are you sure you didn't see him?"

"I might have. But I wouldn't have known him as your uncle. Wait. Was he like you? Was he a bringer of light?"

"Bringer of light?"

"Did he help souls the way you do?"

"Ah. Yeah, he was a medium like me."

"The Unholy One does have the souls of some bringers of light. They're trapped like the others, adding to his power." He hesitated and looked around again. "But he considers you the prize. The Light One."

"Why do you keep calling me that?"

"Do you have any idea how damned bright you are? You're almost blinding. But it's also the name by which you're known. Your coming has been foretold for a long time, my boy, probably even before you were born." The man suddenly tensed up. "That's all I can tell you. I need to move. Now. I've been here too long already."

"But do you..." said Nick.

"The best of luck to you," he said hurriedly, and with that, he disappeared.

CHAPTER TWELVE

NICK HEARD A LOUD LAUGH—MORE of a chortle, actually —and snapped his head to the left. Standing outside of the Café Viking was the same young dude in the baseball cap who he'd been seeing around town. As usual, the guy was staring at Nick, but this time with a devilish grin on his face. Was the guy laughing at him? Nick couldn't recall ever seeing him at school, though now that Nick looked at him, he could very well be older than Nick.

Nick approached the stranger. "Did you say something?"

The guy pursed his lips and studied Nick's face. "I don't know why anyone could consider you a threat. You're supposed to be some great adversary? Hah! You're nothing more than a mere babe." He laughed again.

That was when Nick felt it. Sure, he felt the usual signs —the flip of the stomach, the dizziness, the goosebumps—his body letting him know that there was a spirit nearby. But there was something else. Nick felt a coldness that seemed to seep deep into his very soul, chilling him, sucking him in. A massive weight on his chest threatened to steal his breath, and he felt a despair unlike anything he'd ever known. He felt like he was being pulled deeper and deeper into nothingness. His heart took off like a jet as panic set in. He recalled Charlie's words, *"he sucks the joy right out of you."*

With all his might, Nick tried to push aside the darkness that now engulfed him, and he repeated a mantra that Katrina had taught him in his head. *The light destroys the darkness. The light destroys the darkness. The light destroys the darkness.* He imagined himself surrounded by an eye-blinding white light, a light that came from within himself and spread outward like a giant fan.

With each repetition, Nick felt lighter, closer to his usual self, though his thoughts still seemed muddled. Nick never for once released his gaze from the young man's face. His thoughts cleared as he felt his breathing and heart rate return to normal. It felt as though someone had just removed a heavy anvil from his chest.

The stranger frowned. "Well, I'll be damned. Perhaps I've underestimated you, Light One. But no matter."

There were those words again. Light One. "Who are you?" Nick said, trying to keep his panic from overpowering him. The saliva disappeared from his mouth. "What do you want with me?"

The man's smile was twisted and strange. "You truly don't know? Perhaps they should call you The Stupid One or perhaps The Clueless One. Or maybe simply The Idiot."

Nick didn't need the man to answer his questions. Judging by what he'd just experienced, Nick knew damned well who he was. This was the Shadow Demon in the flesh, and now he looked neither shadowy nor demony. He looked like a kid. But there was no mistaking the darkness and power that emanated from him. Is this what pure evil feels like?

"So, I take it you're Leo?" Nick asked in a hoarse whisper.

The demon's eyes flashed with anger. *"You dare use my name?"* The power of the man's words roared into Nick's eardrums, making Nick cover his ears with his hands. "Apparently, someone's been talking too much. No matter. He shall be dealt with appropriately." He pointed a finger at Nick. "But you, my new friend—you can call me My Lord, for I soon shall be."

Nick's fear welled up inside of him once again, to a point where it was nearly paralyzing. He then willed the light from within him to expand, to envelop him completely, and to shield him from any energetic harm. This was one exercise Nick knew well, as Katrina had repeatedly drilled its importance into his head. Nick could see the light as if it were actually there. The light moved toward the kid/demon, and when it did, he stepped back.

A bitter smile displayed on the demon's lips. "No? You doubt me? You shouldn't. The others learned the hard way." There was distaste in his voice but also, unmistakably, a slight hint of fear.

Nick took a step forward. He was about to tell the man to piss off when a voice behind him startled him.

"Nick? Nick Michelson? Are you okay?"

Nick spun his head around. It was Erin, one of his classmates.

"Huh?"

"You were standing there talking to yourself, and you were swaying like you were about to fall over."

Nick blinked and looked behind him, but Leo was gone. He breathed a sigh of relief. "I'm not feeling all that good right now," he said. "Something seems to have come over me all of a sudden."

"Do you need a lift home or anything?"

Nick turned his head for one last look around. He wanted to make sure that Leo wasn't lurking around somewhere. Nick had to ensure that he would never again let his guard down—now that he knew the murderous Shadow Demon was in Gallowspine Mountains, and that the monster knew who he was.

Nick shook himself. "Thanks, Erin, but I'll be fine. Just got a little lightheaded for a moment."

The concern was evident on her face, which Nick thought was a bit strange, given that he's only spoken to her directly a few times. "If you're sure."

Nick nodded and smiled. "I appreciate it. See you at school."

He turned and headed in the direction of his car. So who should he tell first? Katrina or Nate?

"THANKS TO YOU, we now know a lot more than we did before," Nate said. Nick had phoned him up and had just told him everything he remembered from his frightening encounter with Leo and the conversation with Charlie English. "But I'm unhappy to verify that my intuition was correct. The demon has clearly targeted you."

"When is the conference?" Nick asked.

"In eight days. It appears as though I now have plenty of news to tell everyone. Hopefully, we will find a way to fight this. How did that ghost refer to the demon again? The Unclean One?"

"The Unholy One."

There was a long silence. "Who comes up with these names, I have no idea. The name itself suggests an evil of some sort. To be truthful, Nick, I've never encountered a truly dark entity in all my years of doing this work. Sure, there have been darker spirits from time to time, mostly weighed down by their own guilt or regret, but nothing like this."

"Guilt?" as Nick. "From hurting others?"

"Sometimes, yes," said Nate. "But often, it's their inability to forgive themselves for whatever acts they did while they were alive. This is often the case with the souls we encounter, who are unable or unwilling to cross over into the light. It may be guilt that's preventing them from moving on, and in such cases, it is up to us to convince them to forgive themselves. Or it could be fear of what lies in store for them on The Other Side, especially if they've harmed others while they were alive."

"So you're a medium too?"

"No, I don't see spirits like you. I'm a clairvoyant, meaning I get glimpses of the future and the past, and sometimes, a spirit comes through during my readings. But that's extremely rare. I can't see them the way you can—or the way your uncle could.It's more like they send me flashes of events that have occurred."

"So, is there anything I can do about this, Leo? You have no idea how frightening he was. He scared the shit out of me."

"I can imagine how terrified you were," said Nate. "Remember, this is the being we believe is responsible for the deaths of several members of our community. You said you felt him closing in and trying to drag you down, correct?"

"That's what it felt like—like something or someone was pulling me away."

"But now, because of your encounter with him, we have

direction," Nate said. "Rather than fumbling around in the dark, we have a good idea—thanks to you—of what he wants and how he operates. There are several powerful psychics and witches in our community who, based on what you told us, may be able to figure out how to defeat this demon."

"There are witches?" asked Nick. His uncle had never mentioned witches. "Real live witches?"

Nate chuckled. "Not the cauldron-stirring, broom-flying witches you might be familiar with in books and movies, though I imagine that some of them do indeed stir cauldrons." He chuckled into the phone. "No, Nick, these aren't the evil children-eating witches of Hollywood. Actual witches tend to work for the light, for that which is good, like yourself. You'll find that many witches are also quite psychic, so they are a natural fit in our community."

"I don't know much about witches, except what I've seen in Charmed."

"Ah yes, the three beloved Charmed witches. That television show had the right idea, except that real witchcraft is not as immediate as our media portrays in movies and television. True witchcraft is often more mental than physical, though it certainly can cause changes in the physical world."

"There's so much to learn," Nick said.

"And the learning is never-ending. Until we get back to you, I want you to be extra careful and keep using the protections Katrina taught you—especially the one you used during your encounter with the demon, since it seemed to ward him off. Also, I must ask that you avoid being alone whenever possible. I'm not sure if he'll attack with others around, but until we're sure, you must limit the possibility of you being open, exposed, and vulnerable. It's possible that the appearance of your school chum drove him off for the moment. And for god's sake, don't interact with any ghosts."

"Um... that might be a problem." Nick was silent. Maybe he shouldn't have said anything.

"Nick? Talk to me."

"There's this ghost with whom I've been working. He's the one I told you about—the one who the demon attacked and tried to snatch. I'm trying to get him to cross over, and I think I'm finally getting close. Given that I've invested so much time and energy into these two, I can't walk away now. I really need to see this through."

"*Two*? There are two spirits?"

"No, only one. I meant him and his boyfriend, who is alive. The living one is having a hard time letting go of his dead partner."

"I see." Nate was silent, and then he sighed. "I can't say I'm all that surprised. Katrina told me what a big heart you have."

"She did?"

"Yes." Nate sighed into the phone. "It's against my better judgment, and as I mentioned, I'd prefer that you make no contact whatsoever with any spirits. But since this one has contacted you repeatedly, he'll likely continue to do so, and the more often he does, the greater likelihood of danger there is for you. It may be for the best of all concerned if you can get this spirit to cross. Do what you need to do to make that happen, but if you can get Katrina to help you, all the better. But it would be best if you didn't have any contact with him whilst you're alone. Tell him you'll only speak to him in the presence of Katrina. And it's vital that you be extra diligent with your protections when he's around you, especially if he's ready to cross over. Your life depends on it, young Nicholas."

"I will. I promise."

"I'll contact you as soon as the consortium meets and will let you know what they decide. In the meantime, be careful!"

Once Nick disconnected, he stretched out on his bed, still holding the phone. Maybe Nate was right. Perhaps it would be best to stay clear of any ghosts until this Leo character is dealt with. Nick couldn't get the experience with the demon out of his head. That feeling of hopelessness and despair that he'd felt—it was like nothing he'd ever experienced before and something that Nick hoped he wouldn't encounter again anytime soon.

No, he'd stay away from spirits for now. Tyler and Tony have waited this long. Nick was sure that they could continue on as they have been for a while longer. The next time Tony appears, Nick will tell him that, for both their sakes, he needs to stay away until this entity is dealt with.

Nick felt his resolve harden. It's decided. He will not help any more ghosts—he will not put himself in the way of danger again. He'd been lucky thus far, but if this keeps up, his luck is bound to run out, eventually. Hell, it nearly did today.

No, he would lie low for a while. Spend time with Gabe, study for the end of the semester exams, and be as normal of a kid as possible.

CHAPTER THIRTEEN

NICK STARED AT THE TELEVISION, but his brain didn't register what was playing on it. His thoughts replayed his meeting with Leo over and over and over. He shivered as he recalled the dreadful feeling that came over him from the demon—a feeling that he didn't want to experience again any time soon. His father's voice snapped him out of his reverie.

"Nick?"

"Huh?" Nick blinked and turned his head to face his father.

"Is anything wrong?"

Nick closed his eyes briefly and shook his head. "Not really."

"It's just that you've been awfully quiet tonight. Exceptionally so. I also noticed that you didn't eat much at dinner."

"I'm just kinda tired, that's all."

His father creased his brow. He picked up the black remote that was next to him and turned down the volume.

"Are you sure that's all? Is the new job going okay?" From the tone of his voice, he hadn't been fooled.

"Working at Katrina's is great. It's fun, and so far, the clients have been super cool."

"You know you can talk to us about anything, right?"

Nick moistened his lips and took a breath. "I know. I'm just having a bit of trouble with an especially difficult ghost. He's turning out to be rather frustrating."

His father stared at him for a long moment without speaking. "I see. It's not getting you into any sort of danger, is it?"

"No," Nick lied. "It's nothing like that. It's just a lot for me to try and figure out at the moment."

His father straightened in his chair. "You want to run anything by me? Maybe I'll be able to help. Sometimes it helps to get the point of view from a neutral party."

Nick shrugged. "Not this time, Dad. This is something that I need to figure out for myself."

"If you're sure. We don't mind talking about this with you—your mother and I. You know that, right? We're here to support you any way we can."

Nick felt a thickness rise in this throat. "I appreciate you saying that."

His father cleared his throat and met Nick's gaze. "I'm not only saying it, Nick. I mean it. Don't hesitate to talk to either of us about your abilities. God knows my brother shouldered all of it alone for his entire life." His chest heaved. "I want things to be different with you."

Nick nodded, wordless. He was about to turn his head back to face the television when he felt a whoosh of icy cold air as if opening the front door to a windstorm. A sudden sharp cramp in his stomach caused him to lurch back in his chair. The sensations had caught him off-guard, but he knew their source: ghost.

All at once, the smell of motor oil perfumed the air. It was light but noticeable, and Nick had smelled it before.

Nick slowly turned his head and breathed a sigh of relief, seeing that the ghost in question was Tony and not Leo. He wouldn't know what he'd do if Leo ever showed up at the house.

"Nick, you have to help!" Tony cried out. "It's Tyler!"

"What!?" Nick choked out, momentarily forgetting that his father was in the room. "What's wrong with him?"

"He's... I dunno. There's something wrong. He wrote out a bunch of notes and then tossed a gun in his backpack. He was crying. I think Tyler's going to do something, something to himself. Something bad."

"You're positive about this?"

"It sure as hell looked that way. I felt wave after wave of sadness coming from him. Then he said, 'Tony, I'll be with you soon. Then we'll be together.' Nick, please. You have to do something. You've got to stop him."

Bloody effing hell. Nick's heart pounded in his chest. He snapped his head to look over at his father, to gauge his reaction to Nick talking out loud, seemingly to no one. His father stared at Nick wide-eyed.

"It's a ghost," Nick said. His father gave a weak nod but said nothing.

Nick turned his attention back to Tony. "Where is he now?"

"Doctor's Park."

"The place where you died?"

Tony nodded. "Do you know where it is?" He now looked paler than usual.

"It's not far from here. I could—"

"I think he's going to kill himself," Tony interrupted. Nick could see the tears in the ghost's eyes. "I never wanted that. I never wanted Tyler to die. I only wanted to be with him, to stay with him here. You know?"

"I know."

"Please help him, Nick. You have to stop him from doing this. I have this really, really bad feeling that if he dies, I'll never see him again."

Nick jumped up from the chair. "And you're coming with me," said Nick. "You're the only one who can stop him from doing this."

"Nick?" said his Dad.

"I'm sorry, Dad. I need to go out for a while. It's super important. I promise I won't be gone long."

Nick's father drew a breath as if he were about to protest, but instead closed his eyes and softly nodded. "Do you want me to come with you?"

"No, I need to do this alone."

"Hurry!" cried Tony. "We have to go now!"

Nick looked at his father and nodded. He snatched the car keys off the counter and then turned toward the front door.

"Be careful, Son," said his father before Nick reached the door.

"I will," said Nick. The door snapped shut behind him.

His hands shook as he tried to insert the key in the ignition of his mom's car. He was thankful that she was at home this evening, meaning her vehicle was available. Nick wasn't permitted to drive his father's car, a BMW he'd purchased less than a year ago. His mother still refers to the car as his father's mid-life crisis toy.

The car started, and he peeled out of the driveway. It was dark, meaning that finding Tyler was going to be even more difficult. Nick had been to the park several times, and he remembered that it was enormous. With any luck, Tony will be able to pinpoint Tyler's location.

Nick turned into the long entrance drive to Doctor's Park, where three other cars sat in the parking lot."

"Tony?" he called out. "Are you here?"

Nothing. Dammit. Where was he?

Nick slammed the door once he exited. "Where in the hell are you?"

"Here," a voice said from behind him.

Nick spun around to face Tony. The ghost practically glowed in the dark. "Where is he?"

Tony pointed to the path on the far edge of the lot that led down to the water. It was about a quarter-mile walk to the lake from the top of the parking lot.

"Really?" Nick asked.

"It's where I died. Down there, in the water."

Nick took a deep breath and took off in a run down the path. Because of his inability to see clearly in the dark, he had to slow down his pace to a careful jog, fearing that he could easily sprain his ankle by tripping over a tree root or get smacked in the face with a tree branch. Luckily, Tony's presence next to him created enough light so that Nick wasn't in total darkness and was able to maneuver his way clumsily down the path.

Nick inched his way slowly down the hill toward the lake. By the time he reached the water, he was out of breath from the path's last steep incline. He bent over, put his hands on his knees, and sucked in several lungfuls of air. Nick straightened and looked around. He saw nobody.

Tony appeared directly in front of him and pointed. "There, on the left."

Nick squinted. A little way down along the lakeshore, seated on a log, was a figure.

"Is that Tyler?"

"That's him. He's holding the gun."

Nick lingered for a moment, hesitating to approach an emotionally distraught dude with a gun. Not that it would be the first time he's done that.

"Go on," Tony coaxed. "But slowly."

Nick's heart pounded wildly in his chest. His feet squished as he walked in the wet sand, and he could feel the cold wet of his shoes soak into his skin. Nick could see Tyler clearly now. The gun lay on the log next to him.

Nick swallowed. "Tyler?"

Tyler bolted upright at the sound of Nick's voice. Apparently, he'd not heard Nick's squelchy approach.

"You again!" Tyler said, visibly shaking. "You scared the hell out of me."

"Sorry about that," Nick said.

Tyler narrowed his eyes and glared at him. "What are you doing here?"

Nick studied Tyler's face. Tears streaked his face, and he was blinking like a madman. "Tony told me you were in trouble."

Tyler blinked at him, appearing confused. "He told you I was in trouble? What kind of trouble?"

Nick gestured to the gun with his head.

Tyler let go of an eerie chortle. "Oh, that." His eyes grew downcast and distant.

Nick waited, but Tyler said nothing. "Tony's worried about you. He was afraid that you were going to hurt yourself."

"Why can't you leave me alone for once?" Tyler said, ignoring what Nick said. "Please go."

"Not without you," Nick said. He could almost feel Tyler breaking apart like shards of glass.

"You don't get it, do you? I only want to be with him, my Tony. I know he's with me and can see me, but it's not enough. Then it hit me. If I end my life, then I can be with Tony for good. We can be together again."

"Tell him it doesn't work that way," said Tony, an urgent tone in his voice. "If he kills himself, we'll never get to be together. Ever. He'll end up someplace else, someplace where I won't be able to find him."

Nick briefly wondered if what Tony said was true or whether he was making it up for Tony's sake. Nick decided that it didn't matter.

"Tony's here, Tyler. He said that if you kill yourself, you'll be apart forever. He won't be able to be with you, that you'll both be in two different places."

Tyler's face crumpled. "Hell?" he asked. "If I committed suicide, would I go to hell?"

"Not exactly, but someplace like it," said Tony.

Nick shot Tony a look. "Really?" Nick asked.

"I dunno," Tony said. "Maybe. When I figured out what Tyler was doing, I felt something seriously wrong... something that told me that if he does do this—if he does kill himself—that he'll be lost to me for good."

Nick told Tyler what Tony had said and then added, "Tyler, this isn't the way. It isn't your time yet. You have a full life to live, and you need to live it knowing that you were—are—loved."

Tyler studied Nick's face for a long moment. His shoulders wilted. "It just hurts so damn much."

Nick closed his eyes and nodded. "I know."

"I would have done it eventually, even if you hadn't come along to tell me that Tony's ghost was still here. End it,

I mean. I've been thinking about it ever since Tony died. A lot. I don't want to live without Tony."

"You and I are the same age," Nick said. "We've got our whole lives ahead of us. Who knows? Maybe someone else will walk into your life tomorrow—someone who might never be able to completely replace Tony, but who could fill in some of the void he left behind. I can't imagine what I'd do if I ever lost Gabe, but I know that I'd go on. I'd have to. We have to. Who knows what else the world might have in store for us? Hell, either of us could become famous. Maybe even become a billionaire."

Tyler gave him a weak smile. "How'd you get to be so smart?"

Nick shrugged. "All this crazy ghost stuff makes me see things a bit differently." Nick sat next to Tyler on the log. "I've lost people I care about, too. It does get easier, although I don't think you ever forget them. They're always with us."

Tyler nodded and said nothing. They both stared ahead, listening to the waves crashing loudly and rhythmically on the beach.

"The gun," said Tony, breaking Nick out of his reverie. "He still has the gun."

"So how about you give me the gun?" asked Nick.

"I can't. It's my brother's. He'll kill me if he finds out I've taken it."

Nick was about to say something about the 'kill me' comment, but thought better of it. "How do I know you won't do anything stupid?"

Tyler locked eyes with him. "I won't. I promise. It was only that... I was feeling so lost without Tony. I'd never hurt myself knowing that I wouldn't be with Tony if I did."

"And knowing that you have a full life ahead of you," said Nick.

Tyler sighed. "Yeah, that too."

"Tyler, you —"

"I know," Tyler interrupted. He sighed. "But it's so hard right now—almost impossibly so."

"It'll get better," answered Nick, his voice barely above a whisper. "I promise."

"I really loved him, you know?" said Tyler. "He was the love of my life."

"Tell him I love him more than anything, and I'll always be with him," said Tony. "But I don't want him to push love out of his life. I want him to find someone else someday."

Tony's words surprised Nick, considering how jealous the ghost was initially. Nick told Tyler what Tony had said. "And he wants you to be open to finding someone else to love someday." Nick chucked Tyler lightly on the arm. "There are a lot of cute guys at school, you know."

Tyler smiled. "Especially Jake Ingham."

Nick let out a breath that was part amusement and part relief. "The soccer player? You know, I've always wondered about him."

"You think he might be gay? Or bi?"

Nick shrugged. "Who knows? If not him, there are plenty of others."

Tyler closed his eyes for a moment. "I never want to forget Tony. I don't want this pain, but I'd rather have it than forget about him."

"You'll never forget about me," said Tony. "I'll always be your first love."

"Tony says that you will never forget him and that he'll always have a place in your heart as your first love. You know, Tyler, there's a difference between forgetting and letting go. Letting go of Tony doesn't mean you'll forget him."

Tyler dabbed at his eyes. "Why did you have to go and die, Tony?"

"Believe me, Ty, it wasn't my choice. I should never have..." He stopped and widened his eyes. "Holy shit!"

"What is it?" asked Nick.

"I remember now! I know who was there that day! I was not alone. Connor Burgin was there."

Nick creased his brow. "Connor who? The name doesn't sound familiar."

"He was a year older than me. After Tyler said he didn't want to go swimming, I called Connor. We used to hang out a lot when we were younger, and I felt kind of bad that I'd been ignoring him ever since I met Tyler. But he didn't know I was gay, so because of that, I ended up pushing him out of my life. You see, I wasn't out of the closet to anyone when I was alive. I did go to some gay kids' meeting with Tyler once, but that's it."

"What's he saying?" asked Tyler.

"He remembers who else was there that day."

"He wasn't alone? Who else was there?"

"Someone named Connor..." Nick looked at Tony.

"Burgin," the ghost said. "And tell Tyler that he's very straight."

Nick chuckled and told Tyler what Tony had said. Nick turned his regard back to Tony. "So why didn't he help?"

"He doesn't know how to swim. I'd forgotten about that." He pointed toward the water. "The water is shallow pretty far out, but then there's an abrupt drop-off. Normally, it wouldn't have been an issue. I'm an excellent swimmer. Still, I should have known what was coming. I should have turned around and headed back toward the shore. But I didn't. Stupid, stupid, stupid."

"What are you talking about?" asked Nick. "Why should you have gone back in if you know how to swim?"

"I remember walking out further when I began feeling a bit weird... spacey. Everything was getting fuzzy, and one of my arms got all tingly, like jolts of electricity were running through it. I should have known what that meant. I should have known a seizure was coming."

"A seizure?" asked Nick.

"I was epileptic. I took anticonvulsant medication, which helped to prevent seizures, and for the most part, it was quite effective. It'd been a long time since my last seizure. But I always knew right before one would hit me. I should have recognized the signs."

Nick turned to Tyler. "Did you know Tony had epilepsy?"

Tyler nodded. "He had a seizure once when we were having sex. Scared the living shit out of me. All of a sudden, his eyes rolled back into his head, and he began thrashing about like crazy. I thought he was having a heart attack or something. I was getting ready to call 911 when he came out of it. It would have been nice if he would've told me he had epilepsy before that happened."

Tony chuckled. "Oh, yeah. I forgot all about that."

"So that's how you drowned?" asked Nick. "You had a seizure?"

"Ah," said Tyler. "I never even thought about that possibility."

Tony was silent for a moment. "That's what happened. I could hear someone calling out my name repeatedly. Strange, usually I don't remember anything when I have a seizure, but I clearly remember hearing my name and then seeing Conner standing at the water's edge with a horrified look on his face. Maybe I was already dead, and that's why I remember it?"

Nick shrugged. "Could be. But our brains do work in weird ways."

"You're telling me?" Tony said. "So then I remember seeing him running away, and then everything went dark. Next thing I knew, I was with Tyler, and he couldn't see me."

"But why didn't he report it? Why didn't he tell anyone?"

Tony stared at Nick. "Your guess is as good as mine. It's not like he caused it or anything. I'm guessing it freaked him out too much. Still, I can't believe he didn't tell anyone. I mean, I friggin' died, and he was there. That's weird, isn't it?"

"Agreed," said Nick. "It makes no sense."

"So, what's going on?" asked Tyler. He was staring intently at Nick. "What's he saying?"

Nick filled in Tyler. "So it looks like Tony drowned, but this Connor kid never reported it."

"What? That bastard could have got help!" cried Tyler.

"No, it was too late," said Tony. "I think I was already dead by the time he figured out what was going on. He would never have made it up the path and drove away in time to tell anyone."

"But why didn't he call someone? Surely one of you had your phone with you."

"Have you checked the signal here?" Tony asked.

Nick retrieved his phone from the pants pocket and tapped the Home screen. "Oh. No Signal."

Tony nodded. "Exactly. There was no way to contact anyone." He widened his eyes. "Can you do me a favor, Nick? Contact him and tell him it's okay? Tell him that there's nothing he could have done. If you don't, he'll carry that guilt with him his entire life."

"I will," said Nick. "Does he go to your school?"

Tyler cut in. "Are you talking about Connor? Yeah, he's two years ahead of me. He's kind of a dick."

Tony chuckled. "The only reason Tyler calls him a dick is that he was jealous of Connor. He never understood that Connor was only my friend. For some reason, Tyler thought Connor was trying to steal me away. Didn't matter that Connor was as straight as they come."

"I'll tell him. I promise."

Tony snapped his head to the left. He shielded his hand over his eyes. "What's that odd light coming in off the water? I've never seen anything so bright."

Nick glanced at the water, then back at Tony. "I don't see anything." Realization then struck him. "Ah, it must be your light. Nobody else can see it because the light is meant only for you."

"You mean that's *THE* light?" Tony asked.

"It must be," said Nick. "It's ready for you now."

"What are you and Tony talking about?" said Tyler.

"He sees the light," said Nick. "He's getting ready to leave."

Tyler gasped. "Leave? How can he leave?" Tyler looked up. "Tony, you can't leave! You promised me that you'll always be with me."

"And I will," said Tony. "Wherever I go, I'll always be with you. We'll always be connected."

"He said that he'll always be with you no matter where he is."

Tears ran down Tyler's face. "Do you have to go, Tony?" His voice was cracked and low. "Can't you stay a little longer?"

Nick was about to object, but Tony cut him off. "I can't, Tyler. It's time for me to go. But know that I'll love you always and forever, my little man." He took one last look at Tyler, smiled, and then turned his regard toward Nick. He mouthed the words 'thank you' and then vanished.

Nick breathed a sigh of relief that there was no interference with the crossing—that Leo didn't make an unwelcome appearance. Nick had nearly forgotten all about him up until the moment that Tony crossed.

"He's gone," said Nick, his voice thick with emotion. "He's crossed over."

Tyler stared at him for a moment, wide-eyed. "So it's finally over. He's gone for good."

"Not really," said Nick. He tapped on Tyler's chest. "He'll always be here. Don't ever forget that."

〜

"HEY NICK, IT'S TANA," said the voice on the phone. Nick had called her earlier to ask about Connor. He made her promise not to tell Ericka, given that he'd promised her he wouldn't involve Tana in any more Tyler business.

But this was different. This wasn't strictly Tyler business, though Nick had told her that Connor was a friend of Tony's, and he wanted to ask him personally if he'd be willing to help Tyler deal with Tony's passing. So it wasn't a lie. But he couldn't tell her that he's passing on a message from a ghost.

"Tana. So what'd he say?"

"He was confused, but said he'd talk to you. I didn't mention Tyler's name, just like you asked. I said that you were a mutual friend of Tony's and wanted to ask if he'd be willing to help another friend deal with Tony's passing. Can you meet him tomorrow after school at the bench outside of Café Viking? Do you know it?"

"Yeah, I know it," said Nick. "Tell him I'll meet him there tomorrow at 3:30 after school."

There was a long pause. "Are you sure this is a good idea, Nick? I mean about bringing someone else into this thing with Tyler. I'm kinda concerned about Tyler and the effect it'll have on him."

"Trust me, it's all good."

"I hope you're right, Nick. So how's that boyfriend of yours?"

It still sounded strange to hear someone refer to Gabe as Nick's boyfriend. "He's doing great. And your girlfriend?"

"You tell me. You're the one who gets to see her every day. Now that she's working Monday through Friday after school, I hardly get to see her at all. But we'll have to double again. It was fun last time, despite it being the prom."

"For sure," said Nick. He thanked her again for helping him and hoped that this would be the last time he'd have to bug her. This was the second meeting she'd set up for him with someone from her school.

The next day when Nick arrived at the cafe, a good-looking kid with short-cropped blond hair and glasses was sitting on the bench.

"Connor?" Nick asked.

The kid looked up at Nick and studied his face for a long moment. He nodded. "So you're Nick. We haven't met before, have we? You don't look familiar."

"No, we haven't. I appreciate you meeting me." Nick sat down on the edge of the wooden bench next to Connor.

"This is kinda weird. So Tana said this was about helping someone at our school deal with Tony Fisher's death?"

"It's more about Tony Fisher, actually. You were friends with him, right?"

Connor's jaw tensed, and he paled. "Fisher. Yeah, I knew him. He was my neighbor—we grew up together. So what's this about?"

"I know you were there that day."

Connor reared back. "What are you talking about?"

"The day Tony died. I know he wasn't alone. You were there at the lake with him."

His face flushed with anger. A laugh that was full of sorrow escaped him, but he brushed it off. "I don't know what you're playing at, but this isn't fucking funny."

Nick had no idea whether Connor knew Tony was gay, so he decided to skirt around that fact. "Okay, so here's the thing. I really could care less if you believe me or not, okay? I promised Tony that I'd pass along the message to you, so here it goes. I'm only going to say this once, so don't interrupt. I can see spirits, people who have died but haven't yet crossed over. Tony was one of those spirits that I saw, and I helped him pass on a couple of messages. He told me that the reason he drowned was that he had an epileptic seizure."

"A seizure?" Connor asked. "He had epilepsy?"

Nick ignored him and continued. "Tony understands that even if you could've contacted someone to let them know what had happened, it would have been too late. He drowned pretty quickly, probably before you even realized he was in trouble. He doesn't want you to feel guilty for what happened or for not telling anyone. There was nothing you could have done."

An awkward silence stretched out before them. Nick prepared himself for ridicule, but Connor said nothing. He continued to gape at Nick.

Nick thought that this would be an excellent time to make a hasty retreat. He started to rise when Conner grabbed his elbow.

"Wait," Connor said. "Please."

Nick turned to face him and noticed that Connor's eyes now glistened with moisture. Nick sat back down, saying nothing.

Connor's breath hitched. "Is it really true? You can—like—see ghosts?"

Nick nodded. "Unfortunately, yes. It's true."

"And you saw Tony? You talked to him.... after?"

"Strangely enough, he showed up at the prom. Since I was the only one who could see him, he came to me for help. Well, to be truthful, I went to him. But that's a long story."

Connor swallowed and then sighed heavily. "I dunno. This is some pretty weird shit, dude."

"As I said, it doesn't matter to me whether you believe me. I'm just the messenger. The only reason I'm here is because I promised Tony."

Nick began to rise once again, and Connor said, "No, wait. Please. I believe you."

Nick locked eyes with him and noticed the pained look on his face. He immediately felt guilty for being such a dick to Connor. "I apologize, Connor. I didn't mean to come across like such an asshole. But I'm not entirely comfortable talking about this stuff with people, you know? Especially strangers."

Through his tears, he gave Nick a weak half-smile. "I can imagine." He wiped his eyes with his sleeve. "So Tony told you he isn't pissed at me?"

Nick nodded. "He doesn't blame you at all."

"I know it wasn't my fault he drowned, but I was so

freaked out. I thought about going into the water to try and help him, but knew that if I did, I'd drown too. You see, I don't know how to swim. I never told Tony that I couldn't, but I think he probably figured it out. He never once said anything about it or otherwise let on that he knew, but I'm sure he did."

"Ah, so that's why you didn't try to help him."

Conor nodded. "I've never told a soul about the swimming thing—it's too embarrassing. I do go into the water but never venture out more than waist-deep. That day, however, the water was way too cold for my taste, so Tony went in without me. He was pretty far out by the time I realized something was wrong."

"I imagine that's a scene you'll never forget."

Connor glanced around, as if making sure no one was listening. "I replay it over and over in my head. I don't know why I ran. I was scared—and frustrated. I mean, I should have been able to help him, you know? Once I got back home, I planned to call the cops to tell them what had happened. But then I thought: what if they suspect me? What if they think I killed Tony?"

"Why would they think that?" For the first time, Nick wondered if maybe Connor *did* have something to do with Tony's drowning.

Connor shrugged. "I dunno. It just would have looked suspicious. Think about it. Tony and I are out swimming by ourselves. He drowns, and I just leave him there. How in the hell could I explain that? I couldn't even explain it to myself."

"Tony told me there was no cell service, and I verified it myself when I was there. Even if you wanted to, you couldn't have called anyone until you got home."

Connor raised his eyebrows. "Really? I didn't know."

He lowered his eyes. "But I hate myself for not even checking. Once Tony disappeared under the water, I ran. What in the hell is wrong with me? That's well and truly fucked up."

Nick reached over and touched his sleeve. "It's alright, Connor. Really. Tony forgives you. Though I will agree that not calling anyone when you got home was somewhat of a bone-headed maneuver, but nothing is your fault. Tony doesn't want you to feel bad."

Connor nodded and then leaned in as if he were about to tell Nick a secret. "He was gay, you know. He liked dudes, though I never told him I knew. I saw him a couple of times with that blond kid from school."

"I know."

"How'd you find out?"

"Tony told me all about it. I contacted his boyfriend to pass on things Tony wanted him to know."

Connor studied Nick's face for a moment, and Nick knew that Connor was wondering about Nick, wondering if he was gay as well. *Don't even ask, Connor. Don't ask.*

"Well, I'm not gay," Connor said matter-of-factly. "Not that I care. I knew he was dating that younger kid. I wish he would have trusted me enough to tell me. Instead, he ended up shutting me out and stopped hanging out with me."

"I can't imagine it's an easy thing to do. Coming out, I mean. He was probably afraid it would get out at school somehow, and you know how difficult some kids can make your life."

"I never thought about it that way. Yeah, there are a couple of gay kids at our school who get a lot of shit from others, though I doubt if that would have happened to Tony. Nobody was going to push him around. He was a scrappy bastard."

Nick chuckled. "Yeah, from what I know of Tony, I agree. I'm guessing he could definitely hold his own. He was probably more worried about his boyfriend."

"It was Tyler Tarrant, right? The boyfriend?"

Nick nodded, but said nothing.

"Yeah, I figured. I've seen them together quite a few times at school, and just the way they acted made me think they were a couple. I dunno what it was—maybe the way they looked at each other or something. So it was right about that time that Tony started acting strange around me and made excuses whenever I asked him to hang. I was going to tell him that I knew about him and that Tarrant kid, but figured I'd wait for him to tell me. He never did."

"I'm sure he would have in time."

Connor shrugged. "Maybe." He reached over and tapped Nick on the shoulder. "Listen, I gotta run, but I want to tell you how much I appreciate that you did this—telling me about what Tony said and all. I feel one hell of a lot better than I did. Thank you, Nick."

"You, Connor, are most welcome."

CHAPTER FOURTEEN

NICK PACED the floor of the cottage, occasionally stopping to pull out his phone and check the time. Gabe was supposed to have arrived ten minutes ago, and it wasn't like him to be late. Nick mentally kicked himself for being so nervous, so uptight. It's not like he and Gabe haven't been alone before.

Although it'll be the first time that Gabe and Nick will be alone in the same bed. No, that's not entirely true. They'd been on sleepovers before when they were little. But that was different. This will be different.

Nick walked to the window and pulled back the curtain. No Gabe yet. He sighed, now thinking that his brilliant plan was a colossal mistake. Sure, he and Gabe were boyfriends, and they've made out a few times. Well, more than a few times, actually, and things did get a bit hot and heavy. Nick did not doubt how he felt about Gabe, and believed that Gabe cared for him as well. But was he ready to do the deed?

His dad had once told him during a rushed and embarrassing conversation that once you make love with someone, there's no going back. There's no undo. And that's what Nick was afraid of. What if it somehow changed his relationship with Gabe? What if Nick was shitty in bed, and Gabe wanted nothing more to do with him?

Nick ambled toward the couch and threw himself down on it. He brought up his legs and then wrapped his arms around his knees. No, he wasn't ready. Not yet. He needed to feel more confident, more sure of himself before he slept with Gabe. He'd tell Gabe that they were going to have to wait a little bit longer. Gabe would understand—or at least Nick hoped he would.

He swallowed and once again checked his phone. Gabe was now nearly twenty minutes late. Maybe Nick wouldn't have to tell Gabe that he'd chickened out. Perhaps Gabe had made the decision for him. Maybe Gabe had chickened out himself.

Nick's head snapped up to the sound of a car pulling up to the cottage. Shit. Gabe was here.

Nick stood up, not quite sure what to do with himself. He sat back down, his heart thumping in his ears. He mustn't appear too eager.

A loud knock rang out, and Nick jumped up once again, trying to calm the pounding in his chest. He hoped Gabe wouldn't be too disappointed when Nick told him that he'd decided to wait.

Nick took a deep breath and flung open the door. The sun lit up Gabe's blond hair, and his intense blue eyes glittered. He wore a tight-fitted white t-shirt and jeans. Nick felt Gabe's gaze on him, intense and unyielding. Uh-oh. This was going to be a lot more difficult than Nick had thought. Why did Gabe have to look so damned hot? Nick felt a pulse of excitement.

"So," said Gabe, giving him a crooked smile. "You gonna invite me in or what?"

"Oh, sure. Sorry." Nick stepped aside and gestured with his hand for Gabe to come in.

"You look good," said Nick. *You look good? Was this the best he could come up with?*

"So do you," said Gabe. "But then, you always do."

Nick swallowed hard and shut the door. "Let's sit."

Gabe followed him to the couch, and they both sat down. Nick was relieved when Gabe sat on the opposite end.

Nick drew a breath. "Want something to drink?"

"Nah, I'm good." He met Nick's gaze. "So, how's Tyler doing? You said you crossed Tony over, right?"

Nick nodded. "It was rough going at first, but I think Tyler will be okay. I promised Tony that I'd check in on him. Last time I talked to Tyler, I made him swear that he'd see the school counselor, and he said he would. I hope he does." Nick took a deep breath. "But damn, I thought I'd never get that ghost to cross. I'm just thankful there were no scary unwanted guests."

Gabe creased his brow. "What do you mean?"

Oh shit. Nick hadn't meant to let it slip. He hadn't yet told Gabe about his recent encounter with Leo—but now was not that time. It suddenly occurred to Nick that he's keeping way too many secrets from people—from his parents, from Gabe. This was something that he needed to fix.

"I just meant that since we were at a park—alone and at night—there was a chance that someone creepy might show up and distract Tony enough so that he wouldn't cross. But luckily, it was only us three."

"Ah," Gabe said. He glanced around the cottage, and when he did, Nick noticed a slight quiver to his chin. Gabe was as nervous as Nick was, which strangely made Nick feel better.

Gabe met Nick's eyes. "So we're finally alone," Gabe said. "Here. Just the two of us. No parents. Just us."

Nick's heart picked up speed. *Be still*, he told himself in his mind. "Yeah. Finally."

"Any chance of your folks stopping by unexpectedly?"

"They play cards every Friday night and usually don't get home until late. Not that they'd come here if they were home. Come to think of it, I can't recall them ever coming here on their own. Not one time—though my mom came here once with me to see how things were." Nick ran his fingers through his hair. "I suppose it is possible that they'd come here tonight to check up on us since this is my first time staying here the night."

"Is the door locked?" Gabe asked.

Nick's mouth went instantly dry. Gabe was driving him down the road of no return, and Nick was going to have to decide quickly if he was going to be a willing passenger.

"It locks by itself when you shut it." Nick was surprised at the huskiness of his own voice.

"Then we have nothing or nobody to worry about, do we?" asked Gabe. "Nothing exists right now except for us— you and me."

Gabe flashed Nick a wicked smile and slid closer to him on the couch so that their legs were touching. Gabe took hold of Nick's hands and brought them both up to his mouth. He grazed his lips lightly over them, causing a shiver to creep up Nick's spine.

"Are you sure?" Gabe asked, his voice a whisper.

"About what?"

Gabe pressed his palm against Nick's cheek. "This. Us." He slanted his head slightly to the left. "I don't want to do this with you unless you're one hundred percent positive. I can wait, Nick. Hell, I'd wait forever for you."

Nick felt his earlier resolve weakening quickly. Unable to speak, he only nodded.

Gabe's eyes roamed from Nick's face to his chest, and then back to his face. He smiled, tilted his head slightly, and brought his face toward Nick's neck. He lightly kissed Nick's neck a couple of times and then brushed his lips down toward Nick's throat. Nick groaned.

"So that's a 'yes' then?" Gabe whispered into his year. "Is that what I'm hearin'?

Nick nodded again and let go with a throaty, "Yes." His pulse pounded like a war drum.

Gabe met Nick's eyes and smirked in that way that only Gabe could. Gabe stood up and held out his hand. "How about we move to the other room?"

Wordlessly, Nick took Gabe's hand, and Gabe pulled him up. Hand in hand, they walked towards the small bedroom off of the living room. Before they reached the bed, Gabe stopped, locked gazes with Nick, and then cupped Nick's face in his hands.

"You know I love you, right?" Gabe asked.

"I know," said Nick.

"And?"

"And I love you too."

Nick had been so caught up in Gabe's words that he hadn't noticed Gabe's hands reach around and untuck Nick's t-shirt from his pants. Gabe pulled the shirt up over Nick's head and then tossed it to the floor. Nick tensed for just a moment as he moved faster and faster towards an inescapable decision. Yes, this was really going to happen. There was no stopping it now. Not that he'd want to. Not in a million years.

He stared up into Gabe's smiling face.

"God, you're beautiful," said Gabe.

Nick felt himself flush, and before he could respond, Gabe took hold of Nick's shoulders and pulled Nick close to him. His mouth met Nick's, and Nick's head swam from the pure pleasure of the searing kiss. Sure, he'd kissed Gabe before, but this was something entirely different. There was hunger in this kiss—hunger and need. Nick knew right then that Gabe had won. At this moment, he owned Nick completely, and Nick was okay with that. Really okay.

Gabe's hand roamed down Nick's back as his tongue gently nudged Nick's mouth open. Nick shivered as he accepted Gabe's soft silky tongue and then whimpered as he reached around to pull Gabe even closer to him. His hands seemed to have developed a mind of their own, and they moved up and down Gabe's side and back. He loved the way Gabe's muscles played beneath his fingers.

Gabe broke the kiss, a wicked glint in his eyes, and pushed Nick onto the bed. Gabe fell on top of him, his mouth crashing once again on Nick's. At the feeling of Gabe's hot skin against his, a mixture of fear, lust, and excitement took hold of Nick. From the way Gabe's hands moved over him—tentative yet purposeful—Nick guessed the feelings were mutual.

Gabe's hips rocked against Nick's, and Nick felt wave after wave of excitement rush within him.

"Please, Gabe," said Nick, although he wasn't quite sure what he was begging for.

"I'm gonna take care of you, real good. Don't you go worrying that cute little 'ol head of yours about a thing."

The seductive tone of Gabe's voice made Nick even more desperate.

Gabe reached back, cupped Nick's head and pulled him up, and his mouth covered Nick's. Nick slid his tongue into Gabe's mouth, savoring the heat of him like an exotic dessert he'd never tasted before. Gabe's tongue met his, and they melted together, the taste of Gabe quickly destroying Nick's sanity. This was the feeling Nick had ached for all these years—to have Gabe in his arms. Feeling Gabe wanting him. It wasn't long before the kisses increased in intensity, and their touching became more frantic... more demanding.

Gabe pulled away from Nick, and they locked gazes. Gabe blushed, appearing suddenly shy. He flashed Nick his classic crooked smile and then scuttled down so that his face was even with Nick's chest. His lips then began creating a trail of kisses from Nick's neck to his right nipple. Gabe locked his mouth on the nipple and, while sucking, flicked his tongue across it. Nick cried out as an explosion of pleasure gushed through him.

"So you like that, do you?" Gabe said. Without waiting for a response, he locked his lips on Nick's right nipple, causing Nick to gasp once again.

Gabe's mouth released its grasp, and he began kissing and licking his way down Nick's stomach. Nick shuddered as Gabe neared his belt. Stopping for a moment, Gabe reversed course and trailed his way back up Nick's chest until their lips met. Gabe lightly kissed Nick's lips.

"It doesn't get much better than this," Nick whispered. He felt Gabe's arousal pressing hard against his own, just as Gabe's mouth found his ear.

"Oh, you think so? You ain't seen nothin' yet."

Nick whimpered again. Gabe's fingers traced just along

the edge of Nick's belt line. "And I love it when you make those little noises, Nicky," Gabe said, his voice barely above a whisper. It was the first time Gabe had ever called him Nicky. He liked it.

Gabe nuzzled Nick's neck for several long moments while his hands rubbed gently across Nick's stomach. He continued bombarding Nick's senses with his mouth, tongue, and hands.

"I'm gonna kiss every inch of your body," Gabe said without looking up. "Just so you know."

"Every inch?" said Nick, shuddering at the thought. "You sure about that?"

Gabe stopped and met Nick's eyes. "Oh, I'm sure, believe me. I'm guessing that there isn't one part of you that doesn't taste good."

His lips brushed across Nick, from his neck to his belly button. Writhing, Nick reached for Gabe's dampened hair and ran his fingers through it while taking in all the pleasure that Gabe was giving to him. This is what he'd craved, ached for, needed for so long.

Gabe's hands found Nick's belt buckle, and Nick froze. He closed his eyes and felt Gabe's hands first undoing the buckle and then unfastening the top snap of his jeans. Gabe hopped to the floor and grabbed Nick's jeans at the hip. Instinctively, Nick lifted his hips off the bed and Gabe pulled. He tossed Nick's jeans on the floor and then, in one quick maneuver, undid his own pants. In a moment, they, too, were piled on the floor.

Gabe crawled back onto the bed and slowly lowered himself onto Nick, the tented bulge of Nick's underwear pressing against Gabe's. The jolt of Gabe's hardness grinding against his own sent a delicious shiver through Nick.

Nick could hold back no longer and, with his lips locked to Gabe's, reached down between Gabe's thighs, tucked his fingers under the band, and slipped his hand inside.

"Oh my god, Nick!" Gabe cried.

"This is okay then?" Nick whispered.

Gabe nodded furiously. "Uh-huh"

Nick pulled his hand out, and Gabe gave him a look of someone who had just had their puppy stolen.

"Why'd you stop?"

Nick only smiled and then slowly licked his palm. Gabe's eyes grew wide.

Nick locked his lips onto Gabe's, reached down until he was inside of Gabe's cotton briefs, and wrapped his fingers around Gabe's moist arousal. Nick began stroking, first gently and then firmer, then harder. The more he stroked, the harder and more passionately Gabe kissed him. Gabe started whimpering, first softly, then louder and louder. His breath now came in short, rapid bursts.

"I can't hold it, Nick!" Gabe cried out, and then hot wetness flowed through Nick's fingers. Gabe's body spasmed, and then he fell onto Nick, panting.

Nick looked into Gabe's eyes. They were damp with tears.

Uh-oh. Was something wrong? Was Gabe upset?

"I've never imagined it could be this good," Gabe said, his voice trembling. "Waited my whole life for this. I've waited my whole life for *you*."

Nick cupped Gabe's face in his palms. "Me too."

A warm hand sliding in Nick's briefs caught him by surprise. Nick tensed and shivered, falling into pleasure.

"Do you mind if I try something?" Gabe asked.

"Gabe, right now, you can do whatever in the hell you like."

Gabe withdrew his hand and began tracing a trail on Nick's chest with his tongue. He then got up on his hands and knees and pulled Nick's briefs to his knees. Nick kicked them off, and as Gabe pressed his hand against's Nick's arousal, Nick found it difficult to breathe. What was it exactly that Gabe wanted to try?

Gabe got off the bed, which brought Nick to full attention. Gabe stood at the opposite end of the bed. A wicked grin danced on his lips. He placed his hands on Nick's thighs and slowly spread them apart. He then dropped to his knees. His breath was hot on Nick's legs.

It took Nick only a moment to realize what Gabe had in mind. Gabe took hold of Nick, and Nick closed his eyes and lay back. He grabbed hold of Gabe's shoulders, and his fingernails dug into Gabe's muscled skin. Nick's body tensed in anxiety, waiting for what was to come next.

Nick heard Gabe's sharp intake of breath—and then the most intense feeling in the world swept over him, as if his body had come truly alive for the first time. Unable to control himself, he bucked once, then tried to focus only on the sensation, which grew and grew. That hot, silky wet mouth felt so good, so friggin' good. Nick moaned, and Gabe let loose with a breathless grunt. Nick felt the slow suction, then light feather tongue touches.

"So.... amazing," Nick whimpered.

Nick increased his grip on Gabe's shoulders, and his legs shook. Unable to stop himself, helpless nonsense began erupting from Nick's mouth. Heat burned through his body, building and gathering, reaching a point of intensity that Nick had never dreamed possible. For an instant, Nick couldn't breathe, and then with a breathless growl, his world shattered in a flash of bright light that broke off into a million earth-shattering tremors, and he lost himself in release.

Nick's body spasmed for a few moments, and then he fell limp across the bed.

Nick's eyes were still closed when Gabe spread himself on top of Nick. They remained locked together for several minutes, Nick reluctant to break the spell.

"Nick?"

Nick struggled to find enough breath to speak. "Hmmm?"

"You okay?"

Nick opened his eyes and fell into Gabe's azure gaze. "Better than okay," he said. He laughed, trying to fight off the tears of utter joy that wanted to surface. Gabe drew him close, and Nick said, "I've said it before, and I'll say it again: I'm the luckiest guy in the world."

"NICK?" His father's voice rang from the living room.

Shit. He had hoped to sneak in quietly and avoid his parents until he'd had time to process everything that had happened the night before with Gabe. He felt strange—and more than a bit guilty—facing his parents the morning after his and Gabe's *adventures* at the cabin. Maybe it was guilt in not coming clean with them and telling them about his relationship with Gabe. How would they react? He couldn't even begin to imagine. What he did know was that now was not the time. He wasn't ready for that part of his life to become known. He also believed that if his parents learned about their relationship, that would no doubt be the end of any future sleepovers.

Nick stood in the doorway of the living room and

peeked inside. His father was sitting in the recliner, a book folded on his lap.

"Yeah?" Nick said.

"Ah good, you're home," said his father. "Your night went well? No problems?"

"Huh?"

"Your night at the cottage. Your friend stayed with you, right?"

"Gabe, yeah." Nick tried to fight off the red rising up over his face. He made a conscious effort to keep his voice steady. "It was fine."

"Good. I'm glad to see you're getting some use out of the cabin. It's never good to leave a place empty. A house needs regular upkeep. You've been going there fairly regularly, haven't you?"

"A couple of times a week usually, and it's fine. Everything seems to be in working order."

"Are you ready for your exams?" His father paused and creased his brow. "Aren't they coming up this week?"

There were indeed. But whether he was ready for them was another question entirely. "I guess so. I'm planning on doing more studying today and tomorrow."

His father nodded, but Nick could tell he wasn't really listening to him. There was definitely something on his mind, but Nick sure as hell wasn't going to ask what that was.

"Nick, do you think you and Missy would be okay alone for a few days? I know it's the last week of school for you both, but your mother and I need to take a short trip."

"What do you mean, a trip? Since when do you go on trips without us?"

"A high school friend of your mother's passed away, and the funeral is this week. Your mother was very close to

Lainie and needs to be there. I know you and Missy have exams this week, and we wouldn't think of pulling you out of school. I hope you understand."

"Lainie died?" Nick had known her ever since he was little and called her Aunt Lainie, even though they weren't related.

"Unfortunately, yes. It was sudden—a heart attack."

"Oh, sure. We'll be fine. Is Mom okay?"

"She's taking it pretty hard, as you can imagine. We can get someone to stay here with you both if you like. Maybe Auntie Linda? Or perhaps you could ask your friend, Katrina?"

"No, we'll both be okay. As long as you leave us some food."

His father chuckled. "Of course, we'll leave you food. And some emergency money."

"Cool!"

"With the keyword here being '*emergency*,'" his father said, with a half-grin on his face."

"Got it. So when are you leaving?"

"Monday morning. As I said, we'll be back by the end of the week."

"Where is the funeral?"

"Macon."

"As in Georgia? That's a long way. I thought Lainie lived in Illinois."

"She did, but she married a couple of years ago and moved to Macon."

"Strange that I didn't know that."

Nick turned to go, but his father's voice stopped him.

"Oh, Nick, were you able to help Tyler?"

Nick stopped dead in his tracks and spun back around to meet his father's gaze. "Come again?"

"The other night," his father said. "You said that this friend of yours, Tyler, was in trouble and might do something to harm himself. I haven't had a chance to see you since then."

"I so did not say that."

His father creased his brow. "You didn't say what?"

"Tyler. I said nothing about going to help Tyler."

"Son, you did. You said that you were afraid Tyler was going to harm himself, and then you dashed out of the house."

Nick's heart raced rapidly in his chest. "I made a point of not mentioning Tyler's name in front of you. I never have." Nick hadn't wanted his parents to know that he was working with a ghost and his boyfriend. He wasn't sure why, but he just knew that he didn't want to have that discussion with them quite yet.

"I distinctly recall you saying—"

"It wasn't me." A thick lump rose in Nick's throat, and the realization of what his dad was saying slammed into him. "It was Tony who said that. The ghost. He was the one who said Tyler was in trouble."

His father's eyes widened and his face blanched. His eyes darted past Nick as if he were looking for an escape route.

"You can fucking see them, can't you?" said Nick. His voice was thick with emotion, but now he didn't care. His voice trembled as he spoke. "All this time. You acted like I was the weirdo in the family, like there was something wrong with me. But you can see them too. Like me. Like Uncle Mitch. Like Grandpa."

His father stayed silent for a long moment, and he blinked several times. It was the first time Nick remembered his verbose father at a loss for words. Finally, he broke the silence.

"Nick, you have to understand that I couldn't let your mother find out. She wouldn't have understood back then, especially after what happened between her and your uncle. As years went by, it became more and more difficult to tell her."

Nick found himself involuntarily quivering with anger. "So you pretend you can't see them?"

"Pretty much. They've stopped bothering me, and truthfully, I rarely notice them anymore."

Nick winced. "So when they came to you for help, you refused them?"

"It wasn't like that. I had no choice. Your mother—"

"Not the point," Nick said, cutting him off. "Don't use Mom as an excuse. That's lame. Admit it. You were too chicken to face what you are. Hypocrite."

"Now, you listen here, Nick—"

Tears poured down Nick's cheek. "No! I am not going to listen to you. You are a liar! How could you do this to me? To them? To pretend that I was the only freakazoid in this house? But at least I'm not a *lying* freak like you!"

With that, Nick turned and ran toward the front door. He had to get out of there before he said something that he'd genuinely regret. His father shouted out his name several times, but Nick ignored him and flew out of the house. He ran down the street, turned the corner, and kept running. Once he was several blocks away, he bent over, trying to catch his breath between his sobs.

He hadn't seen this one coming. He wouldn't have guessed in a million years that his father could see spirits. His father's deception felt like a hot knife stuck in his gut. He thought about how his Uncle Mitch had been estranged from the family because of his ability, and all this time, Nick's father was the same. But he just hid it. From Nick, from Mom, from everyone.

What should he do now? He considered going back to the cottage, but that would probably be the first place his dad would come looking for him. Not that Nick was planning on running away or anything like that. He simply couldn't face his father right now. He didn't know what to say to him or how to forgive him.

Still breathing heavily, he stood up and looked around, thankful that there wasn't anyone else around to witness his dramatic display of emotion. He sucked in a deep breath, knowing that he'd have to return home and face his deceitful dad. He wiped his eyes with his sleeve, turned around, and was about to take a step when the coldest, heaviest sensation he'd ever experienced overcame him—a sensation that froze him in place. Adrenaline rushed through him, causing his breath to come in short spurts. Whatever or whoever was causing this made Nick shiver violently, a deep shiver going right to his core. But he had no goosebumps, no flippy stomach. It wasn't a ghost.

So what was it?

Nick slowly turned, and he felt as though he were swimming in a pool filled with tar. His movements were agonizingly slow, and it was only with the greatest of effort that he was able to turn around. It felt as if the world were in slow motion, he included.

In front of Nick stood a hooded figure, clad entirely in black. He wore what appeared to be a wide-sleeved robe that descended all the way to the ground. Nick could not see the person's hands or face, and his arms were crossed over his chest. Or her chest—Nick couldn't tell whether it was a woman or a man. Or neither.

Leo.

No, it wasn't Leo, though how he knew this, he wasn't sure. This feeling differed from what he'd experienced when he was around Leo. With the demon, Nick could sense its evil, its darkness. But this... this was different somehow. It felt ancient and looming and dark. But was it evil? Nick couldn't be sure, but at the moment, he didn't feel threatened, which was strange given that he was immobilized. But whatever this being was, Nick did feel as though he were in the presence of someone or something very powerful.

"Nicholas."

The word floated out from underneath the person's hood in a silent rush and seemed to hang in the air between them. It was then that Nick noticed that the figure hovered in the air, floating several inches above the ground.

"Who are you?" Nick said with great effort. His mouth fought against him as he tried to speak. "Are you a demon? Did Leo send you?"

"I am not."

The figure's words sent another wave of chills through Nick, and Nick felt as though he should drop to his knees, that it was somehow wrong to remain standing. Nick couldn't bring himself to look at the figure's hood, to try and get a glimpse of his face. For reasons unbeknownst to him, Nick avoided the figure's gaze, his eyes locked on the ground.

"What do you want with me?" Nick asked, while staring at the black cement beneath his feet.

The hooded figure ignored Nick's question. "Events are progressing as they should be—events in which your father was not meant to play a part. It is you, young Nicholas. It was always you."

Nick wanted to see the figure's face, but again found himself unable to move. "Me?" he choked out. "What do you mean?"

"You must prepare for that battle that is to come. Events are in flux, still uncertain, and could go either way. The key is your heart's connection."

"What's coming? What do you mean?" His breath hitched in quick spurts, eyes pinned to the sidewalk like looking up might break him. "How am I to prepare?"

"It is not yet time. Soon, young friend."

And as suddenly as it had appeared, the being was gone, and Nick felt as though he'd just been freed from quicksand. He had never experienced a feeling of such utter helplessness before. With the demon named Leo, Nick felt as though he could handle himself. But this demon—or whatever it was—was different. The power coming from it was something Nick had never encountered before and would prefer not to experience again.

But Nick knew he hadn't seen the last of the hooded figure—and if the guy was telling the truth, a serious shitstorm was brewing, and somehow, it was up to him to get ready. But how? Hopefully, Katrina, Nate, or some of Nate's friends would know.

But now, he had to do something that he couldn't put off.

He had to return home and face his father.

In the next book, Nick and Gabe are out camping when Nick encounters a confused ghost who looks familiar. Much to Nick's chagrin, the ghost follows him home and won't leave him alone. Want to find out more? Grab your copy of

Camping with a Ghost, Book 5 in the Ghost Oracle
series now!

Thank you so much for supporting my work! If you'd like to
stay up-to-date on upcoming releases and sales, then join
my weekly newsletter (which also includes a short story
every week!)

Newsletter: http://rogerhyttinen.com/newsletter/

A NOTE FROM ROGER

If you enjoyed *Ghost at the Prom*, I would love it if you let your friends know so they can experience Nick's ghostly adventures as well. If you leave a review on the site from which you purchased the book, Goodreads or your own blog, I would love to read it! Email me the link at
writerdude@wisguy.com

If you'd like to be notified when I release new books and receive a short story in your inbox every week, please sign up for my newsletter at http://roger-hyttinen.com/newsletter/

Thank you so much for supporting my work!

Questions? Comments? I'd love to hear from you! Contact me at:
writerdude@wisguy.com

CONNECT WITH ME

Visit the link below for my newsletter, including exclusive stories, bonuses and advance notice about upcoming work.

Subscribe To My Newsletter: **https://roger-hyttinen.com/newsletter**

Connect with me:

Follow Me On BlueSky:
https://bsky.app/profile/artful-dodger.bsky.social

Like Me On Facebook:
https://www.-facebook.com/rogerhyttinen.author/

Visit My Blog:
https://rogerhyttinen.com/

CHECK OUT MY OTHER BOOKS

Standalones

A Touch of Cedar

Christmas Cookies that Sparkle

Pushed under the Mistletoe

Ghost Oracle Series:

Nick's Awakening (Ghost Oracle Book 1)

Anaconda! (Ghost Oracle Book 2)

The Magician's Secret (Ghost Oracle Book 3)

Ghost at the Prom (Ghost Oracle Book 4)

Camping with A Ghost (Ghost Oracle Book 5)

Nick's Destiny (Ghost Oracle Book 6)

Wolves of Norbury series:

Norian's Gamble